nobody else
has to know

Other books by Ingrid Tomey

The Queen of Dreamland

Savage Carrot

Grandfather's Day

Neptune Princess

nobody else
has to know

INGRID TOMEY

ACKNOWLEDGMENTS

My thanks to these good people: to Officer Dan Clark, whose expertise in
accident investigation was invaluable; to Nick Brigulio, who shared the
pain of his accident with me, and to Doug and Kathy Brown and Abby for
doing the same; to Dr. Jerry Rosenberg and his office for helping me once
again; to my DWW writers' group for insight and encouragement; and,
finally, to my wonderful editor, Wendy Lamb, for caring so much about
this book.

Published by
Dell Laurel-Leaf
an imprint of
Random House Children's Books
a division of Random House, Inc.
1540 Broadway
New York, New York 10036

Visit us on the Web! www.randomhouse.com/teens

**Educators and librarians, for a variety of teaching tools, visit us at
www.randomhouse.com/teachers**

ISBN 0-440-22782-8

RL: 5.5

Reprinted by arrangement with Delacorte Press
Printed in the United States of America
November 2000
10 9 8 7 6 5 4 3
OPM

*For Grampa, who was always a hero,
and for Paul, who loved him*

chapter 1

WEBBER SPRINTED down the sidewalk, in no hurry to get home but too full of energy to slow down. He loved the feel of the sidewalk unrolling beneath his feet, of everything pumping inside him. Autumn leaves lifted and spun in his wake as he dodged around clumps of other kids making their way home from Spratling High.

"Hey, Webb!"

He glanced over his shoulder and flipped a hand at a bunch of kids from Heffner's class.

"How'd you do on the algebra test?" Jeff Scott yelled after him.

"Aced it!" he yelled back.

Snorts of laughter followed him down the sidewalk.

"Sure you did, Freegy. We all know what an Einstein you are!"

Webb just grinned and kept going, feeling the sweat break under his shirt. The day was warm, but he couldn't stop long enough to put his books down and take off his jacket. He shot around a bunch of girls waiting for the walk signal at Washington. In front of the bakery he passed Dylis Clark handing out blue flyers. She knew better than to offer him one of her "Global Alerts"—harangues on rain forests or dolphin populations.

One of the bakery's big garbage cans had rolled across the sidewalk. Webb cleared it, barely breaking his stride. Behind him he heard Dylis say something, but he didn't look back. In the next block, on his right, an orange sawhorse stretched across someone's driveway. Webb veered into the street and charged the sawhorse full tilt. Right leg forward, left knee tucked, he sailed over the top and landed in the driveway, sinking slightly into asphalt. That was when he realized the sawhorse was there to keep people off the freshly surfaced drive.

"Ooops!" He looked down at his black footprints and then up at the windows of the house. Nobody had seen him. He darted onto the next lawn. An old black Lincoln pulled up next to him.

"Boomer!"

Webb stopped. "Grampa!" He jogged over to the car and smiled at the white-bearded face leaning out the passenger-side window. Tossing his books on the grass, he flopped down beside the Lincoln and pulled off his canvas jacket. "Hey, guess what?"

"What?" His grandfather looked down at him. "What is it, Boomer? Did you get kicked out of school for breaking too many hearts?"

Webb laughed and picked up a wooden button that had come off his jacket. He tossed it up in the air with one hand and caught it with the other. Then he slid it back into his pocket for his mother to sew on.

Grampa stuck his arm out the window and rapped the side of the car impatiently. "What?" he said. "Stop horsing around and tell me."

"I ran the sixteen hundred in four-thirty."

His grandfather sank back in the seat and smacked himself on the cheek in amazement. "Say 'Honest to God.'"

Webb nodded. "Honest to God, I did, Grampa. Coach timed me himself. He said he knows I can best that in the spring and . . ." A slow smile spread over his face. "I'm leading everyone, even the seniors."

"Ha-haaa!" Grampa reached over to the wheel and honked. Passing kids stopped talking to stare at the thin, white-haired man. "I knew this was our lucky day, Boomer." He closed his eyes. "Yesterday," he said, opening them again, "yesterday, I could hardly raise these bones from my bed. Barely had the pep to even lift a coffee cup to my mouth. I'm telling you . . ." He pointed a knobby finger down at Webb. "After your mother left I just closed the blinds and lay there, wondering if I'd make the obituaries by—"

Webb groaned. "Grampa."

Grampa held up his hand. "But today I could feel the difference. The instant I woke up I felt the blood coursing through these veins like a young man's. Like a soldier's when he's going into battle." He sat up straighter in the passenger's seat and began reciting his favorite poem. " 'Forward, the Light Brigade!/Charge for the guns!' " he said. Grampa was bellowing, waving his arm out the car window at startled passersby. He looked back at Webb and shook his fist in the air. " 'I got plenty to live for,' I says to myself. And was I right? Look—my grandson, famous, an overnight sensation."

Webb grinned and shook his head. Grampa was acting like Webb had won an Olympic gold medal. But Webb didn't really mind.

"Mark this day, Boomer. You're gearing up for the four-minute mile. I'll see you run it before you're twenty, believe me. Did I tell you?"

"Yeah—one or two thousand times." Webb stood and held up his hand to high-five Grampa, but Grampa grabbed his hand between both of his own and kissed it. Webb quickly blocked the scene from kids strolling by. His grandfather still kissed him like he was a four-year-old kid. He opened the car door. "Might as well give me a ride home."

Grampa slid back to the driver's seat. "We're going to

4

celebrate." He started the car and made a U-turn, heading back down Market Street the way Webb had come. "From the time you were a little baby I knew you were going to be a runner," Grampa said, pointing a finger at Webb. "I took a look at your legs, even when you were in the cradle. I saw those wiry little legs."

Webb nodded, only half-listening. He waved out the window at a cluster of girls, the ones he had passed at the curb. Maxie Gallagher waved back. She had been over the other night to drop off some drapery measurements for Webb's mother, who did sewing from her shop, Chessie's Needles. Too bad they didn't have cheerleaders for cross-country and track, he mused, imagining coming out of the four-forty to a cheering Maxie Gallagher in a red Spratling sweater.

"By the time you were ten," Grampa was saying, "you could already run faster than Peter Pockets over there across the street."

"Peter Pocknis," Webb said. "No, I couldn't. He could always run faster than me. Except today. I beat him by a whole second. First time."

"Phhh." Grampa took both hands off the wheel and waved Peter Pocknis away like a bad smell. "Remember that time you were four and we were waiting for your father at the airport and you spotted him and broke away from us before anyone could stop you? Nobody ever saw a four-year-old run like that. Your father . . ." He shook his head. "He should be here to see you."

5

Webb nodded, feeling his mood slip a notch. Then he leaned forward and switched on the radio. "Where we going, by the way?"

Grampa's face brightened. "Out to Pembrook Mall—Darvey's."

Webb stared at him. "What?"

"Don't tell your mother. But I'll be damned if you have to wait till Christmas for some decent running shoes."

"Man oh man, Grampa, those shoes cost over a hundred dollars."

"Hundred and thirty," Grampa said. "So what? You're gonna be famous. And they'll look at me and say, 'There's the grandfather of Webber Freegy, walking down the street. You know Webber Freegy, the kid on the Wheaties box? Well, that good-looking gentleman, except for the eye . . .'" He put his fingers over his left eyelid regretfully. In contrast to the deep brown of his right eye, this eye was covered with the thick, milky film of blindness—a result of a childhood accident. "'. . . he's the one who bought Webber his first pair of decent shoes.'"

Webb wasn't really surprised that Grampa would spend so much on a pair of running shoes for him. His grampa's love was one of those things he could count on, like the sun coming up every morning. Grampa would do anything for Webb. With that thought, Webb glanced out the windows on both sides of the car. He and Grampa were on the other side of town on Midline

Road, between fields of wheat on one side and a bunch of spotted cows on the other. "Hey, Grampa, there's no one around. How about letting your famous grandson drive?"

Grampa eased up on the accelerator and pulled over. Webb jumped out and jogged around to the driver's side, rapping his knuckles on the hood as he passed. When Grampa slid over, he got in, wiping his sweaty palms on his jeans. He grinned at Grampa. "I'll be a pro by the time I take driver training in March."

"Don't tell your mother," Grampa said, putting a cigarette in his mouth. He didn't light them anymore, just put them in his mouth when he got nervous.

Webb rolled his eyes. "Oh, right. First thing I'm going to do when I get home is tell Mom I drove Grampa's car all by myself." Webb looked over his shoulder, looked in the rearview mirror and the sideview mirror, and put the car in Drive. He was a little shaky. He hadn't driven more than four or five times.

"You're oversteering, Boomer. Oversteering. It'll stay on the road practically with no help from you. Let her go, loosen up."

Webb took a few deep breaths and loosened his grip on the wheel. He hunched his shoulders up and down and sank back into the seat. Better. He stepped on the accelerator, and the big car shot forward. They passed a boxy green threshing machine chugging through a field of wheat, cutting the grain and flinging it in the air. His eyes returned to the road, leaving the wheat hanging there in the sunlight. Off to his right was another scene—an American flag made from red, white, and blue bricks that some farmer had built in the middle of his cornfield. *The Lemon Lake Daily* always took pictures of it for the Sunday magazine when they were hard up for news.

"I love that," Grampa said, pointing with the cigarette.

"Pretty corny," Webb said.

"No, it's not," Grampa said, not getting the joke. "It's beautiful that he has so much respect for the flag. When I was a kid at St. Mary's I raised the flag every morning; never once in six years did I let it touch the ground. Reverence. Me—the son of poor immigrant parents—I could tell these kids today a thing or two about reverence." He tapped his cigarette on the dash, wiped some stray tobacco off his lip, and put it back in his mouth. "You know, Boomer, I saved that school single-handedly from burning down. It was a very heroic act for a six-year-old. Did I tell you?"

Webb nodded absently. He was really getting the feel of the open road, the surge of power he got whenever Grampa let him drive. He turned up the radio and started beating on the wheel as he sang along, " 'Lay it down, oh, lay it down, put it with forgotten things-s-s-s. . . .' " Spratling had the best track and cross-country team in Michigan, and he was their top runner. It had taken him an entire summer of running laps and leaping hurdles, but he had done it. He was part of something important. Maybe he was barely squeaking by in algebra, maybe he wasn't the social kingpin of the sophomore class. But he could run. Fast. Maybe Grampa was right. Maybe today was the beginning of something big. He rolled down the window and mooed at a cow. Life was sweet.

"Webb!"

He looked up and felt wildly for the brakes. He had drifted onto the shoulder and was headed right for a little girl on a red bicycle. Her eyes, wide with horror, stared directly into his.

chapter 2

*T*HE BRICKS *were tumbling, tumbling, tumbling. Red, white, and blue. White, blue, and red. Falling and rising against the blue sky, like colored birds. Soundless as vultures. Festive-looking, his mother would have said. But they chilled his heart as he ran through the mown fields, made him want to jump the fence and run the other way. And all around him the smell of cut wheat like fresh, sweet grass. So sweet he wished he could stop running long enough to taste it. But that was too weird. He wasn't a cow, was he? Cows didn't run this fast. He could feel the bottoms of his feet hitting the stubble of cut grain, a stone, sliding across slick spots where water had gathered. Besides, he couldn't stop. He couldn't stop running. He could never stop running. Never.*

Creaking sounds in his head. Like something in his

brain needed oiling. Webb opened his eyes and saw a big lady with dark brown skin pushing a cart past him. He closed his eyes.

"Honey?" He felt her hand on his arm. "Are you there?"

He opened his eyes again and looked at the smooth dark skin. Gingerbread lady, he thought. Was he still in that place of flying bricks? She smiled at him and he didn't feel so worried.

"Are you back here in the land of the living, Webber Freegy?" She laughed. "You just hold on until I get your mother."

He couldn't help it. He closed his eyes again. He wanted to sleep; he wanted to sleep for a hundred years. He didn't care about his mother. He only wanted to sleep. He could hear her talking. But who was she talking to? The gingerbread lady?

"Webber, open your eyes. It's me, honey. Oh, Webb, please, please wake up. Just look at me for one teensy little second. Webb?"

Webb opened his eyes. It was his mother, all right. Curly brown hair the color of his. Blue eyes the color of his. Same nose. But why wasn't she at work? And she looked like she was crying. He opened his mouth, but nothing came out.

She shook her head forcefully. "Don't," she said. "Don't try to talk, Webb. Just look at me. I just want to see you with your eyes open."

He looked. Blinked. Looked. There she was sitting

11

on the edge of his bed, holding both his hands. But it wasn't his quilt with all the colored patches, the one she had made him when he was small. It wasn't even his room. The walls were ugly, the color of snot. No dresser. No picture of his father. No nothing. He swallowed and looked back at his mother.

"You're in the hospital, honey. Did you know that?"

Then he noticed the tubes running from his hand to a machine beside him. How was he going to run with all this stuff hooked to him? He half-lifted his head. "How—" He stopped. The noise that came out wasn't his voice. It wasn't anyone's voice. It belonged to a bear.

"Shhh, shhh," she said, putting her cool hand against his cheek. That soothed him, made him want to sleep again. He could always run tomorrow.

"Don't worry about a thing," she said. "I'm going to wrap you up and take you home." The last thing he heard was her bright, clear voice singing a silly old song. From when he was little and she used to dance him to bed.

Dancing with my babe-e-e
It almost makes me craze-e-e

The next day or whenever it was, he woke to his mother's voice talking to someone. The voice wasn't growly and deep like Grampa's. It wasn't booming like his father's. Of course, it wasn't his father's. He opened his eyes. He was looking at a man with a pointy brown beard, reddish skin, small glasses. White coat. One of those things hanging around his neck. A doctor.

"He's awake." His mother took Webb's face between her hands and kissed his forehead.

"I'm Dr. Rosenberg," the man said, crossing his arms over his chest and looking at Webb. "How are you feeling?"

Webb nodded. "Okay. I guess." He sounded hoarse.

"Leg giving you pain?"

Now he saw his leg, a white log hoisted in the air, hanging in some kind of sling. He realized that he had been feeling a steady, penetrating pain there all along.

"You busted it pretty good," the doctor said, grinning. "Fortunately for you, I've always liked jigsaw puzzles."

Webb stared at the doctor.

"Well," the doctor said, stepping forward to pat Webb on the shoulder, "you'll want to talk to your mother." He glanced at Webb's mother. "At least, she wants to talk to you." He nodded and disappeared out the door.

"Can you talk?" She squeezed his hand.

"Yeah," he said dully. "My leg."

"Does it hurt?" She moved to the door. "I'll get the nurse."

"Mom." He called her back. "What happened? How

did I break my leg?" He couldn't run? When he had worked so hard, busted his butt all those months?

She hesitated, ran her fingers through her short curls. She came back to sit next to him on the bed. "Do you remember anything?"

He stared at her blue eyes looking back at him. He stared till he couldn't see her anymore. Something clicked in his head. "The bricks," he said. "Those red, white, and blue bricks. I thought they were going to stay in the air. But they fell, didn't they? On my leg?" He looked at her for confirmation.

She half-smiled and shook her head. "Is that all you remember?"

Webb closed his eyes and thought hard. "Maybe it was a cow," he said, describing the picture in his head. "A very . . . very . . . very big cow," he said, drawing the words out slowly. "It must have stepped on me when I fell down. A cow with brown spots." He opened his eyes, looking at her again. There were worry lines across her forehead. "That was wrong, wasn't it?"

She nodded. "It's okay. The doctor said you might not remember."

He groaned.

"What?" She leaned over him. "Where does it hurt?"

She looked from him to the wall and Webb followed her eyes. A monitor displayed all kinds of readouts from machines connected to him by wires and tubes. A jolt of fear made him lurch forward. "What—What is all this?"

She took his hand. "You're okay, honey. Really. Those are just to check on all your body parts, but now that you're conscious they'll unhook you from everything. And we'll get you out of here." She brought his hand up to her cheek and squeezed it. "Oh, Webb, you scared me; you frightened the wits out of me. You just lay there for three whole days. You don't know what it means to hear you talking again. Everyone is so relieved. Your whole running team came to the hospital after the accident. Of course the doctors wouldn't let them come up, so I made them stand under your window and sing the Spratling victory song for you." She laughed. "Beefy too. It was enough to wake the dead. Oh, lordie." She slapped her forehead. "What a stupid thing to say."

All the talking was making him exhausted again. It was funny about Beefy singing, but Webb could only manage a small smile. He wanted to go back to sleep, but something didn't feel right. He closed his eyes, and a little sparkler went off in his brain, a tiny flash of awareness. He opened his eyes. "Where's Grampa?"

"He's home," she said, looking away from him, out the window at the parking lot.

Grampa should be there, Webb thought. If he knew Webb was hurt, nothing would keep him away. "What's wrong with Grampa?" He grabbed for his mother's hand.

15

Her blue eyes searched his face. "He was hurt too. In the same accident as you. But not badly. He has two broken ribs."

He sank back on the pillow and closed his eyes again. "What accident?" he said. Or maybe he only thought it.

The next time he opened his eyes it was dark outside his window, but his mother was still there, sitting beside him. Or maybe it was the next day. It was strange, he thought, to see her just sitting there, not sewing pieces of something together or hemming pants or those other things she did with needles. Her hands were always busy. But she sat there now, her head turned, looking out the window, her hands folded. Not moving.

"I remember what happened," he announced calmly.

"Great," she said, turning to face him. She took his hand. "Tell me."

He nodded, pleased that this news cheered her up so much. "We should have been buckled in."

"Yes, you should have been," she said hotly. "After all my preaching, I can't believe you didn't buckle up—either of you."

"The man told us to," Webb said. "That was the last thing he said—'Buckle up.' "

The frown crossed her face again. "What man?"

"At the Ferris wheel," Webb said. "He told everyone who got on, 'Buckle up, buckle up, buckle up.' But we were eating that pink stuff—cotton candy. We had our hands full, see, me and Grampa, and we didn't listen. Mom, when we got to the top it was so neat—you could look down and see millions of people all wearing gold hats that shone like a million lights, gold lights that lit up the whole world. And when we stood up we could see all the way from Fatty's Funland to Balaklava.

"Balaklava," he repeated, faintly recalling it was one of Grampa's distant battlefields. He smiled at his mother, but she wasn't smiling back. He could tell she didn't believe him. "You think I made that up?"

She shook her head.

"I didn't. I don't think I did," he said, feeling confused again. "I was so sure this time." His head hurt; so did his neck, his teeth, his jaw. "It all came to me when I was asleep."

"It was a dream," she said softly. She took his hand and squeezed it. "Just a dream." And she smiled so he knew it didn't matter.

He closed his eyes, but he thought of something else. "Mom?"

"Mmm?"

"Why were you crying?"

She didn't answer for a second.

"Did you think I was going to die?" He laughed out loud even though it hurt his stomach.

There was another long silence. "I was worried. I was just . . . so worried about you."

"I'm okay, Mom."

"I know." She sighed and added, "Thank God."

Webb closed his eyes. Then he opened them. "How did Grampa break his ribs?"

"In the accident—the car accident," she said patiently.

"Oh, yeah." He nodded slowly, trying to recall something, some tiny detail.

He slept on and off, waking when the nurse came in to check his tubes or change his sheets, sliding him over to one side of the bed and then the other, talking with his mother, washing him all over like he was a two-year-old. Later, he said to his mother, "Was I in the car with Grampa? Is that what happened to my leg?"

"Um-hmm." She patted his hand. "Four days ago now, on Midline Road. You could have been hurt much worse than you are," she added. "You were very lucky, Webber, both of you."

He tried to concentrate. "Did it have anything to do with those bricks?"

"Bricks? I don't think so, honey." She let go of his hand and went to the window. After a few minutes she looked at her watch. "I guess I'd better—"

"Wait," he said. "Wait." His thoughts were clumsy, but he wanted to figure this out. This feeling he had, this awful, unsettling feeling. "Tell me everything," he said. "Everything about the accident."

She slid her wedding ring up and down her finger, looking out at the parking lot. She nodded, turning back to him. "The car hit a little girl riding a bike—

Taffy Putnam, her name is. She's at the university hospital in Ann Arbor."

Webb groaned.

"Grampa is sick, absolutely sick, Webber. I don't think he'll ever drive again. He just sits around and—" She looked at Webb's face and stopped. "Oh, darn, you don't need to hear all this right now."

"Oh, God." Webb put his hand to his head, trying to shut out the pain, trying to blot out the image of the big black car running over a little kid. She was probably stuck full of tubes too, maybe worse than he was. He took his hand away. "Is she hurt bad?"

She sighed and looked at the floor. "She's alive. That's about all we know."

His heart dropped like a stone. "You mean she might die?"

His mother nodded.

"And Grampa's responsible?"

She nodded again.

"Oh, God," he said. "Poor Grampa."

chapter 3

"THERE'S A policeman coming to see you this morning." The nurse, whose name was Zobah, spoke to Webb as she shoved over a vase of flowers to make room for a pot of mums on the windowsill. All the space on the sill and on his bedside table had been taken over by flowers and get-well cards. Zobah surveyed them approvingly and then turned around to look at him.

"Huh?" He stared back at her.

"A policeman," she repeated, raising her voice a notch like he was hard of hearing. "You know, Webber, the man in blue. He wants to ask you some questions. Dr. Rosenberg gave the okay, if you're up to it."

"What for?" Webb tried to sit up. With the tubes

removed from his neck and nose he had a lot more mobility, but he still couldn't sit up without Zobah's help. "Questions about what?" he asked as she slid another pillow behind his back.

Before she answered, Zobah strapped the blood-pressure cuff around his arm. She glanced sideways at him. "It's those extra juices you've been snitching off the night cart. Someone reported you."

Webb didn't smile. He felt a little quiver of worry in the pit of his stomach. "What's a cop want with me?" he said impatiently.

"Oh, it's just about your accident, Webber. They ask you how it happened, time of day, who you were with, etcetera. They always do that, checking everything out." She patted his arm. "Don't look so worried." Squeezing the bulb attached to the pressure cuff, she took a reading. Then she glanced at the remains of his breakfast tray. "You on a diet?"

"Yeah," Webb said. "I've given up eating cardboard." Complaining to Zobah about the food was something he did every morning, but this time there was no fun in it. He slumped back against the pillows. How could he talk to a policeman about something he didn't remember?

Zobah *tsk-tsked* as she pumped up the pressure cuff again. "Didn't your mother ever tell you about the starving children in—"

"Boomer!" Grampa, his white hair flying, pushed into the room.

21

Seeing Grampa, Webb felt a rush of emotion so strong that tears stung at his eyelids. At that moment there was no one he wanted to see so much in the entire universe. "Grampa," he said, holding out his free arm.

Grampa glanced at Zobah and went around to the other side of the bed. Holding his ribs with one hand, he slid the other behind Webb's head and pulled him against his chest. Webb's arm went around Grampa's waist. He felt the stiffness of Grampa's shirt against his cheek, breathed in the smells of laundry starch and his lime-scented soap. He took a deep breath. "I missed you, Grampa. I really missed you," he said. All the pain and confusion of the past few days had been made worse by Grampa's absence, by not being able to talk with him about what happened. Now he was here, his arms around Webb. Now Webb could get through it, even the disappointment of missing cross-country. With Grampa here, everything was okay again.

Grampa stepped back and looked Webb up and down, his eyes taking in the broken leg, Webb's head wrapped in a big bandage, the tubes in his arm. Grampa started to speak and couldn't. He shook his head and swallowed. "My God." He took a deep breath and turned away for a moment. His eyes lit on Zobah. "This is my grandson you got here," he said gruffly.

Zobah nodded. "I figured it out." She undid the cuff. "You know it's not visiting hours till one." She glanced at her watch. "You're four and a half hours early."

"I know, I know." Grampa held up a hand, still cradling his ribs with the other. "I had to get here before that Meals On Wheels dame comes over with my lunch. If I'm not stretched out on the bed with a sheet pulled up to my chin, she'll report me to Missing Persons." He looked back at Webb. "Your mother's got the food cart coming for me every day now."

Zobah put her hands on her hips and faced him like she was getting ready to toss him out the door.

"Listen," Grampa said, sounding suddenly weary. "I'm only staying a few minutes." He leaned on the bed's footboard for support. "I got a cab waiting."

"Cab?" Zobah and Webb both said it at the same time. Nobody in Lemon Lake took a taxi anywhere. If they were carless, they either called up a neighbor or they stayed home.

"Had it sent over from Bolton. Meter's running downstairs."

Zobah nodded. "A few minutes. We've got business to attend to in here." She went out.

"God, Grampa—a taxi? That'll cost you a fortune."

Grampa shrugged, and then, holding his ribs with both hands, he eased himself down next to Webb on the bed. "I could care less. Think I'm going to lie around eating Mrs. Whatsit's potpies while you're in here all busted up like a pretzel? Damn, I haven't looked at your face in five whole days. What a nightmare—not knowing if you would ever walk again, if you would even wake up. Aaah." He pulled his hand down his drawn face and grabbed hold of his beard. "I would have crawled over here on my hands and knees." He let go of his beard and reached for Webb's hand but stopped, groaning loudly.

"You hurting, Grampa?" Webb took his hand and squeezed it.

"Yeah," Grampa growled. "But not in the ribs. What's a couple busted ribs, a busted nose?" He reached up and touched his bulbous nose. "I've had busted ribs before, busted eye, busted lung, plenty of battle scars." He shook his head. "But nothing like this."

"What about—" Webb stopped. It scared him, the idea that the little girl was hurt so badly that she might even die. It made his mouth go dry with fear. He started over. "So what have you been up to?"

"Staring at the walls, staring at the ceiling. Worrying about you. Broken tibia, broken fibula, broken zibula—your leg like a box of cornflakes. 'Spratling loses budding track star.' Headlines on the sports page. Made it sound like we buried you." He shook his head.

"I'm coming back, Grampa."

"Yep. Just like General MacArthur." Grampa rubbed his hands together enthusiastically. "I know you will, Boomer." He looked around the room. "They treating you okay? Those nurses aren't abusing you, are they?"

"Nah." Webb shook his head. "I'm just sick of this place. People poking me, rolling me over, looking at my private parts. Yecch. I'd like to yank everything out and start running. Down the hall and out the door. Just keep going for about ten miles." He pictured it for a moment—leaping out of bed in his hospital gown, racing down the gray-tiled hallway, down the stairs, through the streets of Lemon Lake, past Porky's Diner, the Hollywood Market; the sun on his face, knees pumping. The sweet, tangy smell of cider as he ran past Denzel's Mill, bees buzzing in the air around him, leaves crunching underfoot. He gave a bitter laugh. "I'd like to be able to walk to the toilet."

Grampa nodded. "Your coach called the other night. He feels real bad about losing his best runner."

Webb swallowed. "Yeah?"

"Said he expects you to show up in spring for track."

"Tell him he can count on it. My doctor says I'll be in this cast a couple of months, then I'll have a walking cast, plus I have to go through some therapy stuff, but they always tell you longer than it really is. I'll be running by February, just watch."

"Hell, I know that," Grampa said. "At least February. You got strong bones. Heal fast. Look how you came back from the dead."

There was a long moment of silence. Webb took a deep breath and said it. "What about that little girl?" He could hear Grampa wheezing, and he thought of his one lung gasping for air, like a fish in a bucket.

25

"She's still conked out, five days now. Nobody knows. Gotta say some prayers, Boomer."

They never said prayers, either of them. That had been Webb's father's department. His father had been the churchgoer in the family, the one who prayed when someone was sick, in an accident. Hanging around a post of Webb's bed at home was a black rosary that had belonged to his father. Webb had never used it. "Geez," he said, "is she, I mean, do you think she's going to die?"

"She just might. The little girl might die. It's dicey," he wheezed. They were silent. "Could go hard on me if she dies."

"What? What do you mean?"

Zobah came in and pointed at her watch, and Webb held up a finger, pleading for another minute. She went out.

"Negligent homicide. They put people in jail for less. Remember Ossie?" Grampa sighed heavily.

Grampa had told Webb many times about his friend Ossie, the druggist, who was put in jail for accidentally blowing up his family by experimenting with chemicals in his basement. Webb had an awful image of Grampa wearing his black pants and white shirt, black wing tips, sitting on the end of a narrow bunk in a gray cell, eating a bowl of thin soup. "How could they put you in jail? You weren't drinking or anything." His grandfather never drank anything stronger than Coke. Didn't even drink a beer on a hot night like his mother did. "You

26

weren't driving recklessly." He didn't know that for sure, but his grandfather was the pokiest driver he knew. "Were you?"

"Hell, no," Grampa said. "I never drive over the limit."

"So why would they prosecute you? You're not some crazy drunk driver. The streets are full of crazy drunks. Like that guy who plowed into Kevin Harkness and his mother. He was so drunk he couldn't even walk a line. He only got six months. Why don't they throw the book at guys like that instead of decent, law-abiding old men?"

Webb realized he was talking so much because he didn't want to hear the details of the accident. It made him shudder. Something he was part of but not part of.

"I ran her over, pure and simple, Boomer. She was pedaling down the road, just off the road, innocent as a butterfly. I drove off on the shoulder. Didn't see her. Didn't see her in the least. Careless." Grampa took a deep breath. "It was worse than careless—taking my eyes off the road like that. Hit a little baby, knocked her clean through the air. I saw it one second, saw her frightened little face. But I hit the brakes too late. The reflexes of an old man. We went sliding off the road, down the culvert there. Tipped over like a beetle. You went flying one way, I went flying the other way. Bodies flying through the air." He stopped, panting like an old dog. "You remember this, Boom?"

It was like a scene from a movie. Webb couldn't believe he was part of what Grampa had described. But before he could answer, Zobah showed up at the door again, this time with a policeman.

"The officer is here," she announced, looking pointedly at Grampa.

"What?" He scrambled to his feet. "What are you doing here?"

The officer, who was more than six feet tall and built like a football player, nodded at Grampa. "Mr. Freegy, good to see you again. I've come to speak with your grandson about the accident."

Grampa looked back at Webb. "He doesn't remember anything. Do you, Boomer?"

Webb shook his head.

"You could have saved yourself a trip," Grampa said with a little edge to his voice.

The policeman smiled patiently. "It's just a formality. Just a few questions—I won't stay long. I know your grandson's been through a lot this past week."

"Damn right," Grampa said, letting go of his ribs to rest his hand on Webb's shoulder.

"I guess you're on your way out," the policeman said, nodding at the door, still smiling.

Grampa looked as though he was going to argue but thought better of it. He looked down at Webb. "They're kicking me out, Boomer. Don't worry about not remembering anything—that's not a problem. It happens all the time."

"Okay, Grampa."

Very gingerly, holding his ribs, Grampa bent over and kissed him. "I love you, Boom."

"Me too, Grampa."

Grampa walked out slowly, his head bowed, followed by Zobah.

"Hi there, Webber." The policeman stepped forward and stuck out his hand. "I'm Officer Mike Clark, Accident Investigation."

Webb extended his left hand, since his right one was hooked up to the tubes. "Do you know my grampa?"

The policeman nodded. "I talked with him earlier this week. We investigate all accidents. My department does nothing but that. It's just routine—nothing to get excited over."

Webb shifted in the bed. Was he investigating so he could put Grampa in jail? What if Webb said something wrong, something that might hurt Grampa?

The cop looked around the room. "Lotsa flowers in here." He smiled and sat in the chair next to the bed. "Looks like you got a few friends."

"Yeah, a few." Webb sized the guy up. Six-foot-plus, big all over, in no hurry despite what he told Grampa. "Honest, I can't remember anything," Webb said.

"Ummm." Officer Clark nodded and took out his pen and a spiral-bound notepad. "Your full name?"

"Webber D-Day Freegy."

"Deeday? Like *D-e-e* . . ."

"Like D-Day. The invasion of Normandy."

"Ahah." He wrote it down. "You were born on June sixth, is that it?"

"No." Webb didn't feel the need to tell him he'd inherited his middle name from his father, who was born on June sixth. "My birthday is September twenty-fourth."

Officer Clark looked up. "How old are you?"

"Fifteen."

He wrote Webb's age down, then asked where Webb lived, his mother's full name, where he went to school, ordinary information a cop could have looked up. People did that when they wanted to warm you up, Webb thought. Like salespeople on the phone: "Sure is nice weather we're having, isn't it? A nice mild spring like this makes you forget all about that tough winter, doesn't it?" Then, *blam*—"How about shelling out fifteen thousand dollars for some new storm windows?"

Officer Clark asked, "How old is your grampa?"

"Seventy-five."

"Any infirmities—heart condition, diabetes, epilepsy, narcolepsy?"

"No."

He looked up at Webb and smiled. "You know what narcolepsy is?"

Webb shrugged.

"Listen, Webber. I know you feel it's your duty to protect your grandfather, but you're not going to hurt him by being truthful. When I talked to your grandfather, he was very cooperative, surprisingly so, in fact. It's my job to talk to everyone who was in the accident."

"How about that little girl?" Webb said hotly.

The cop didn't look annoyed by the question. "She's not conscious yet," he said, continuing to write. "Where were you and your grandfather going when the accident occurred?"

Webb blinked. He hadn't thought to ask Grampa. "I don't know."

"Do you remember anything? The scenery? Weather? When you struck the bike?"

"Nothing," Webb said truthfully.

"What kind of driver is your grampa?"

"He's careful," Webb said. "He never goes over twenty-five miles an hour. And he doesn't drink."

The cop looked at him. "Well, we can tell from the skid marks he was going a lot faster than twenty-five."

Webb caught his breath. "How fast?"

"Fifty, sixty. But the limit out there on Midline is fifty-five, so he wasn't breaking the law. Does he generally go that fast?"

Webb was confused. He wanted to say whatever would help Grampa, but he didn't know what that was. "No," he said. "Usually he goes slower than the speed limit. But I mean, he could have been going that fast. I guess."

"You remember the impact? Tipping over?"

"No. Only what my grampa told me."

"Makes it harder to investigate when you tip over. And when the ambulance comes along and scoops up all the bodies before we have a chance to look at things." He clicked his pen and stuck it in his shirt pocket. "But your grandfather has been very cooperative." He stood up and shook hands again with Webb. "You drive, yourself?"

Webb shook his head. "I'm only fifteen."

"Oh, right. Well, take care of that leg. I hear you're a runner."

Webb gave a wry smile. "I *was* a runner."

"You'll come back," Clark said, and went out.

"Me and General MacArthur," Webb murmured.

chapter 4

*H*E WAS *running down Midline Road. The red, white, and blue bricks were chasing him like a thick swarm of bees. Soundlessly they closed the distance, even as he ran faster and faster. That's why he didn't see the car. Only the bricks overhead, ready to attack him, crush him. But it wasn't the bricks that got him. It was the car—big, black, long as a hearse. Coming right at him.*

Webb woke, gasping for breath, his hands over his face. He looked around the ugly green room filled with flowers from his friends, boxes of candy, cards. Against the wall were two brown vinyl chairs—one stacked with the sheets that the morning nurse would put on his bed. He looked at the clock. Seven-thirty. His mother and Grampa wouldn't be here till noon, but he was ready. His jeans with one leg cut off, his U of M sweatshirt, one sock, and one tennis shoe were placed on the other brown chair.

He sat up, slid over to the side of the bed, and reached for the crutches. His armpits ached from the pressure of all the crutching he had done the day before. Lying around in bed for almost two weeks, he had lost much of his strength. He had to toughen up, build up his upper body like the therapist said. Plant and swing, he coached himself, moving slowly down the hall, trying not to look pained. He stopped at the nurses' station and gave them a thumbs-up.

"My, my—King Crutch," said Zobah, stepping out to block his way. "Just crutch yourself right back to two-oh-one, young man. Your breakfast tray is coming around the corner."

"Oh, terrific," Webb said, glancing over his shoulder. "Belgian waffles with fresh strawberries again?"

"No," she called after him. "Since this is your last meal, we ordered you smoked salmon and caviar."

Webb grinned. Bantering with the nurses was the only thing about this place he was going to miss. He went back into his room and sat on the bed, feeling like he had just run the sixteen hundred. Why was he so tired? And he had lost weight besides. His left leg looked like a broom handle. Lifting his cast with both hands, he slid back into bed. He smiled at Gail, the girl with the breakfast tray. She had graduated from Spratling a year ago, and she was already married and had a kid. Even so, she was pretty cheerful.

"Chow time," she said, peeling back the wrap from his scrambled eggs. She gave him an extra orange juice and went out.

Webb started eating his eggs, not really hungry, not even tasting them. For some reason he was thinking about Gail's little girl. Her name was Kelly. Gail had showed him a picture of this little kid who had two teeth and was sort of cross-eyed. Not even that cute. It was the idea of having a little kid like that who might be pedaling down the road in a few years and get mowed down by a big old truck or something.

He shook his head, wondering why he was thinking of something so stupid. Maybe it was the dream that had brought it on. He hated that dream with the flying bricks. If he had to dream about the accident, why didn't he just dream it the way it happened? But it wouldn't come back to him. He couldn't remember even a little sliver. One second he was running down the sidewalk, and the next—*blam*—he was in the hospital. What happened to that chunk of time?

He picked up a piece of toast and chewed it half-heartedly. Grampa probably had dreams every night about what happened. Maybe his were worse. To actually see the car you were driving plow into that little girl. . . . "Poor Grampa," he said out loud, pushing back the tray. He sighed. No sense lying in bed moaning about it, though. For all he knew, that little girl was all better now, turning cartwheels down the street.

For the rest of the morning Webb did the exercises the therapist had showed him—leg lifts with his good leg, knee-to-chest bends, ankle curls, pull-ups on the overhead bar, isometric exercises. He got out of bed and started walking the halls on his crutches again. The therapist told him he'd probably have to use a wheel-chair, "for public distances," like at school and if he went to the mall. But he didn't want to look like a total feeb. It might be tough at first, but he was already stronger on his crutches than he had been a couple of days ago. He'd be able to handle the school hallways with a little more practice.

He stopped at 233 and saluted an old guy who'd had part of his foot amputated two weeks ago. He sort of reminded Webb of Grampa. Grampa had taught Webb how to salute when he was two years old.

"Hey, Beauregard." Hank saluted Webb back. The name was another thing that reminded Webb of Grampa. Hank called Webb Beauregard because he had a dog named that. Grampa's calling Webb Boomer made just as much sense. There was a famous old-time hockey player named Bernie "Boom Boom" Geof-frion. Webb had played hockey when he was seven years old for about six weeks and hated it, even though his dad and Grampa had gone to all kinds of trouble to set him up in a peewee league, with all the best equip-ment. He quit playing, but Grampa never stopped calling him Boomer. Not that Webb minded. He didn't even mind Beauregard.

"Hey, Hank," he called back. "I'm going home today."

"Lucky devil," Hank said. "Take care of that leg."

"Yeah, I will. Take care of your foot."

"Sure thing. I'm taking it home in a box. Giving it to Beauregard." He started cackling.

Webb laughed and turned back to his room. He loved people who could laugh at their troubles. He pictured Hank carrying his foot in a shoe box and giving it to the dog for a chew toy. He laughed again.

His mother and Grampa showed up at seven past twelve, after he already had his lunch tray. But he was prepared to starve rather than eat another mangy hamburger in a big dried-out bun. His mother started helping him get dressed.

"I can do it." Webb took his undershorts from her. "They showed me how to dress myself."

Grampa snatched the shorts from his hand. He held them up and looked over at Webb's mom. "What the devil are these, Francesca? Cactuses?"

"Aren't they cute?" she said to Webb. "Hot off the presses."

"Yeah, adorable." He didn't mind that his mother made all his undershorts because they were pretty cool, with horses or astrological signs or flags on them—nothing cheesy like sunflowers or straw hats. But he

37

didn't want it advertised all over the hospital. He glanced at the doorway to see if anyone noticed Grampa holding up his undershorts. "Let's get going," he said to Grampa. He let Grampa slip the shorts over both legs and up under his hospital gown. "Okay," he said. "I can take it from here." Bracing one foot against the mattress, he lifted his butt and pulled the shorts the rest of the way up. It felt good to be dressing for home. "Oh, no," he groaned, looking at the jeans Grampa picked up from the chair. "Did you have to cut the leg off my favorite pair?"

His mother turned away from the windowsill, where she was putting the flowers and cards into a box. "Sorry, but the others were too tight. They wouldn't have gone over your cast."

"When you get this off"—Grampa thumped on the cast—"I'll buy you a dozen pairs of jeans. Hell, I'll buy you fifty pairs. Who cares about a lousy pair of blue jeans? You could have lost your leg permanently." He licked his lips. "Did I tell you about my buddy who lost a leg permanently?"

He had told Webb a thousand times.

"Took a grenade at Omaha Beach. Yep. Archie Tippett—my pal next door—went off to war, while I stayed home with my bum eye. You coulda lost that leg, Boomer. You coulda been a vegetable for the rest of your life. So let's not have any moaning about blue jeans."

As Grampa helped him slide the jeans up over his

38

feet, Webb glanced at his mother, and she shook her head, which meant he should shut up about the jeans. It also meant something else. He shouldn't ask about the accident, about the little girl. He had a feeling the kid wasn't out of the hospital turning cartwheels. He knew she must be on Grampa's mind, probably all the time. He wanted to say something to cheer Grampa up. But maybe Grampa didn't want to talk about it. Maybe he just wanted to forget it happened for a little while. That was sort of the way Webb felt too. He wanted to get home, go back to school, get healed, and start running again. Things would clear up in time. The little girl would get better, he was sure of it. He zipped up his jeans and snapped them. "Hey, can we stop at McDonald's on the way home? I'm starved for a real hamburger."

"Nope," his mother said. "Lunch is waiting for you at home. Grampa made your favorite meal."

Webb stood up and reached for his crutches. "You made blowtorch chili without me?"

"Grampa's been doing all the cooking without you," his mom said. "And I must say it's been delicious. Last night we had pork roast studded with garlic cloves."

"Don't talk about my cooking, Ches. It's unmanly to be a good cook. Unless you're a great cook. C'mon, Boomer, let's blow this joint."

Webber rode down in a wheelchair, which his mother pushed while Grampa carried the box of flowers and other things. Grampa complained all the way. "I don't know why we have to haul all this stuff home. Just give the flowers to the nurses. And who cares about candy? He needs meat. Meat will put . . ."

Once in the car, Webb tuned him out. Now that he was going home, he started thinking about school, about how behind he was in his classes. And about his friends. He had called Beefy a few times on the phone, and he'd gotten about two dozen cards from other kids and teachers, but he felt nervous. It was like he was a new kid starting school for the first time. Stupid, he told himself. He'd been gone less than two weeks. But things had changed. He couldn't walk. Almost as bad, he couldn't run. He felt like he had let everyone down, especially his team. He needed to get his strength back, show them he was still Webber Freegy, who could run the sixteen hundred in four-thirty. But was he? How long before he could run that fast again?

His mother glanced back at him. "You okay back there?"

Webb shrugged. "Just thinking about everything I have to do. Homework and stuff." He leaned forward. "Hey, who's hanging your drapes for you?"

She laughed. "Beefy. We worked out a deal. He helps me out for a while, and I sew shirts for all the guys in his band."

Webb groaned. "Six shirts. You got the worst of the bargain." Then he started to laugh. Beefy never did anything for nothing. He wasn't the type of guy who'd show up on your doorstep in the middle of a snow-storm to shovel your walk. He might show up, but he'd charge you the going rate. He was a good guy, though. Beefy had sent Webb three cards in the hospital and called Webb's mom every night to see how he was doing. "Good old Beefy," Webb said, looking out the window.

People were in their yards, raking up the last of the leaves. It was a sunny Saturday, so people were out in droves, weeding, washing windows, bagging leaves, getting everything done before the cold weather hit. He saw two kids on horseback. Grampa spotted them too because he started reciting "The Charge of the Light Brigade": " 'Half a league, half a league,/Half a league onward,/All in the valley of Death/Rode the six hundred. . . .' "

Webb couldn't believe it was the first of November. He felt like he was coming back home after traveling in a distant country. Everything looked different. The grass was dying. The trees were bare. Had anyone raked the leaves in their yard?

He got his answer when they turned onto Scott Street. The blue lake glimmering in the sun was the first thing to catch his eye. The second was Beefy in the front yard, raking leaves. Webb rolled down the window and shouted, "Hey, Beefsteak, good to see you doing some honest work for a change."

Beefy threw down the rake. "Heya, Spider Webb—

you finally flew the coop, huh?" He came over to the car, wiping his hands on his belly, and grinning from ear to ear as usual. "You want me to carry you inside?"

Besides being fairly fat, Beefy was strong. He could have done it easily, but Webb handed out his crutches. "I can walk, man. Stand back." He slid his cast out and eased himself down on his left leg while Grampa got out of the front seat, took the crutches from Beefy, and handed them to Webb.

"He's doing great," Grampa said to Beefy. "He doesn't even need a wheelchair, do you, Boom?"

Webb shook his head and started for the front door. Plant and swing, he told himself, plant and swing. He was sweating, feeling the unevenness of the lawn beneath him. This was harder than he'd thought. He could feel everyone looking at him, afraid he would fall. And then the top of his crutch missed the sidewalk, just catching the edge of it. He started to go over. His mother screamed. Beefy caught him, picked him up, and carried him into the house.

"Oh, Beefy," his mother said, following them inside. "Thank God you caught him."

"I would have caught him," Grampa said irritably. "I was right there. I wouldn't have let him fall."

"Put me down, you big oaf," Webb said. He was grinning, but his face burned as Beefy deposited him on the sofa. He was exhausted. Suddenly he didn't care about sitting around talking to Beefy; more than anything he wanted to take a nap. "My hero," he said, punching Beefy's big shoulder and lying back on the pillow. For a brief moment before he fell asleep, he wished he was back in the hospital, back in the ugly green room, safe and sound.

chapter 5

WEBB STILL wasn't used to waking up in his room. He lay there for a second, half-expecting to hear the clatter of the hospital breakfast cart rolling outside his door. He propped himself up on his elbows and then gradually pulled himself up to a sitting position. His legs hurt. So did his head. He had tried to catch up on his homework the day before, but after a few hours he got a headache and couldn't concentrate. He never used to get headaches, he thought, stuffing another pillow behind his head for support. His eyes were drawn to the poster on his bedroom wall that his father used to have hanging in his workshop: YOU ONLY LIVE ONCE, BUT ONCE IS ENOUGH IF YOU DO IT RIGHT.

His father had done it right, Webb thought. He was decent and generous and thoughtful. He might yell his head off when he was mad, but he didn't waste time complaining. Webb's mother had given him the poster after his father died and he had pinned it above his dresser. It was how he wanted to live his life too. Doing it right. He hated having a broken leg, hated hobbling around on crutches, having Grampa or his mother help him dress and undress, wrapping a garbage bag around his leg every time he showered. But, he thought, it could be worse. Like Grampa said, he could have no leg at all. Or, like Hank in the hospital, no foot. "No complaining," he said out loud, throwing off his blankets.

He looked at the picture of his father on the dresser. He was in his football uniform at the University of Michigan. Twenty years old then and big, bigger than Webb would ever be. Big hands, big shoulders, big smile. Big heart. Webb was little like his mother, with small features, light brown hair, blue eyes. So different from his dark, laughing father. But Webb could run. Every time he ran, he imagined his father looking down from the picture on the dresser, cheering him on. Sometimes Webb worried that his father was disappointed that he had given up hockey when he was seven and that he would never become a football player. He looked at his father's picture and promised, *I'll be the best runner at Spratling High, maybe even in Michigan. Just as soon as I get my cast off.*

He was doing his hip extensions in bed when Grampa came to the door. "Beefy's gonna be here in half an hour. I'll help you with your shower."

Webb groaned. "Geez, Grampa. Beefy's my buddy and all that, but did Mom have to hire him for my bodyguard?"

Grampa sat on the bed, holding his ribs with both hands. "Uhhh," he said, settling himself. "You've used up your quota of accidents, she says. You may as well humor her, Boom."

"But she can't afford to pay Beefy." He lifted his left leg perpendicular to the bed and held it there, counting. "Seventy-eight, seventy-nine, eighty." Then he said, "I know she fell behind with her business when I was in the hospital. And I'm not helping out anymore."

Grampa stiffened. "I'm helping out. It's not as if I moved in here to suck up your mother's money."

Webb shook his head quickly. Grampa was so sensitive. "I don't know what Mom would do without you around."

"That's right." Grampa stood up, hitching up his baggy black pants. He looked down at Webb. "She needed a man to take care of her after your father died. And you, too. Naturally I could never fill his shoes." He exhaled, a shuddery sound. "Your father, Webb. He was my boy, and yet, it's like I'm talking about Robert E. Lee. He was a hero, Webber. A true-life hero." Grampa walked to the window and gazed at the lake, placid and blue in the dawn light.

Webb started his isometric exercises. With the slightest encouragement, his grandfather would go into the whole story of how his father died to save a drowning man. Webb wasn't up for it.

He loved Grampa, couldn't imagine living without him, couldn't imagine coming home from school and not seeing him in the middle of the living room in his black pants and white shirt, reading about the great battles. He knew his grandfather loved him more than anything in the whole world.

Webb had been eight when his father died. Grampa took Webb out of school for three days and drove him down to Tennessee, to Fatty's Funland. He let him go on any ride he wanted as many times as he wanted, bought him an endless supply of hot dogs, french fries, and slushies. It was a sunny, warm week in March, and Webb rode the Cyclops over and over. He remembered the feel of his stomach rising up to his throat with every plunge, remembered screaming with laughter. It seemed to him then that his laughter filled the entire park, the seats of the Ferris wheel, the toss-a-dime booths, the tent with the snuffling baby pigs.

At night, they would go back to their little motel room, and Grampa would sit at the window, staring out at the night, more silent than Webb had ever seen him. Webb would lie in bed with a blanket over his head, thinking about riding the Cyclops the next day, trying not to think about what his grampa might be thinking about. Webb could never have gotten through that time without him. Grampa was the best, Webb thought, but he hadn't exactly rescued them after his father died. Webb and his mom had been on their own for four years. Then Grampa had surgery and his lung was removed. Webb's mom made Grampa move in so she could look after him. And it bothered Webb how Grampa always talked about Dad like he was somebody Webb didn't know. Grampa made him sound like someone in a book, some mythic hero or some soldier leading a charge into battle, into the valley of death. But for Webb, his father was the big, laughing man who stood in his undershorts in front of the bathroom sink and let Webb spread shaving cream on his own face, who took Webb to Mass every Sunday morning and then took him out in the fishing boat in the afternoon. I don't need Grampa to tell me about my own father, Webb thought, as he pulled a sweater over his head.

Grampa handed him his crutches. "Okay," Webb said, heading down the hall. "Back into the real world."

When Beefy pulled up, Webb was waiting on the front porch with his crutches, leaning against the railing, watching the little kids march by on their way to his old elementary school. He could feel Beefy, his mother, and Grampa watching him move slowly to Beefy's old Buick, waiting for him to make a fatal slip.

"Be careful," his mother called. "Don't forget to use the wheelchair for long distances. Beefy, stay right with him."

"He's all right," Grampa growled. "He's tough."

But as Beefy dropped the folded wheelchair in the trunk, Grampa called, "Don't forget to lock the seat of that chair, Beefy. Stay out of crowds."

"Whew," Beefy said as they pulled out of the drive. "I feel like Nurse Jane Fuzzy Wuzzy."

Webb moaned a little as he tried to get comfortable in the backseat. "Shut up. I don't know what my mom is paying you, but remember, this job is only temporary."

Beefy chuckled. "Gas money, only gas money, Webb." He switched on the radio and started singing along with Nasty Dogs. " 'Sleet in my hair, sleet in my hair-r-r,' " he bellowed. " 'Why do I wai-ai-ai-t . . .' "

Beefy played drums in a band called Dark Secret. He played wicked drums, but he couldn't carry a tune in a bucket. Webb started singing along, glad to be distracted. He had mounds of homework he hadn't finished, and he was already tired just from getting ready for school. How was he going to get through all his classes? " 'Why do I wait,' " they sang, " 'when you're never th-ere-ere-ere? . . .' "

They pulled up in front of the old redbrick building that was Spratling High, and Beefy turned off the car. "I'll get the wheelie."

"Forget it," Webb snapped. "Just hand me my crutches when I get out." He concentrated on looking at ease as he made his way up the sidewalk with Beefy beside him, wheeling his chair.

49

"Hey, Webber. Long time no see," a kid from English class yelled.

"Hi, Den," Webb called back, taking his eyes from the sidewalk and wobbling a little.

"Uh, uh, uh, uh," Beefy chided him. "Baby steps, remember?"

Webb made it to the big double doors. A girl from algebra class ran up and held one of them open for him. "Hi, Webb," she said, smiling. "Welcome back. How's your leg?"

"Well, my left one is great," he said, and she giggled as he moved past her.

When they got to the door of his homeroom, Beefy said, "I'll leave this thing in the hall and meet you back here at nine-thirty."

Webb nodded, wishing Beefy had homeroom with him. He felt a little dazed by all the activity—lockers slamming, kids yelling, throwing their books through the air. Had he been part of this only two weeks ago? He inched forward as the door opened, and Mr. Annelin stepped out, holding the door for him.

"Well, Webber," he said, gripping him by the shoulder, "we heard you were coming back today. C'mon in."

Webb walked in, and everyone started clapping. He looked back at Mr. Annelin, wondering what they were applauding for. Then he saw the huge banner across the back of the room. WELCOME BACK, WEBBER! He blinked and looked around at all the smiling faces, kids cheering. They were cheering for him. The banner was for him. His mouth dropped open and he started to grin, half-embarrassed, half-pleased.

"Hey, Webber, we missed you." Annie Gully came up and hugged him.

From behind Annie came Maxie Gallagher, her dark hair shining under the fluorescent lights. "Hi, Webb," she said, crinkling her nose at him.

"Hi." Webber absorbed her hug awkwardly, with both arms still attached to his crutches. It was a good thing he was holding them, he thought. If he'd had his hands free, he probably would have crushed her. Maxie Gallagher didn't hug him every day of the week. She had never even brushed her pinkie against him.

"Can I sign your cast?" she asked, holding up a Magic Marker.

So far the only person who had signed his cast was his mother. Grampa had refused, saying, "It's unmanly to let people write on your leg." But with Maxie standing two inches away in her pink angora sweater, smiling at him like he had just returned from battle, Webb said, "Oh, sure, yeah," and dropped into a chair that Mr. Annelin pulled over for him.

"Uh-oh," she said as she squatted down beside his leg. "Somebody beat me to it." She turned her head to read what his mother had written down the length of his cast. " 'Buckle your seat belt.' " She laughed and shook her head. "I'll bet your mother wrote that."

When Webb nodded she rolled her green eyes.

"Mothers are put on earth to torment their children: 'Eat your spinach.' 'Be back by eleven.' 'Buckle your seat belt.' "

"Yeah," he said, grinning. "Yeah, that's my mom." He watched, holding his breath, while she wrote: "You're even cuter on one leg than you are on two— xoxoxoxo, Maxie."

After Maxie finished, everyone else lined up to sign his cast. Mr. Annelin didn't object; when everyone was done he borrowed a marker and signed too.

Webb usually sat in the back row, wising off with the guys, not really participating unless he was called on, not even paying attention half the time. But now, in every class, the teacher had a special seat for him in front so he wouldn't have to walk so far and risk tripping over someone's feet and also so he could sit with his cast propped up on another chair. Everyone wanted to sign his cast. And they wrote things that amazed him, like "Way cool, Webber," "I missed you, blue eyes," "Heal fast, Speedball!"

Peter Pocknis came up during lunch and slapped him on the back. "Webber, you big oaf. We finally get a chance at state champs, and you go and bust your leg. Way to go, gimpy."

Webb looked up from his sandwich. Peter was almost six feet tall and dressed like he spent a half hour choosing his clothes every morning. His khakis were creased; his plaid shirt matched his green sweater. His tasseled loafers shone. Webb tried to disguise his irritation by thinking of a witty response. He swallowed the rest of his tuna fish, but before he could open his mouth Maxie Gallager stopped with her lunch tray.

"Oh, right, Peter. He goes out and breaks his leg on purpose so he can sit on the sidelines and watch *you* lose to St. Regis."

Peter flushed. "I didn't lose without a lot of help. Look at Jaster's time. And Phipps fell."

Webb grinned at his tray. For years Pocknis had out-distanced him. He was president of the drama club, drove his own Mustang to school, and dated every good-looking girl. And he never missed an opportunity to rub it in. "Well, Pocknis, you're right about one thing," Webb said. "If I'd been there, we would have beat Regis, no sweat." He reached up and punched him in the shoulder. "Don't worry. I'll be back in the spring, better than ever."

After Peter moved off to the next table, Maxie took a piece of cake off her tray and set it in front of Webber. "Here, I brought you some carrot cake. I was afraid it would all be gone by the time you made it up there. If you need anything else, just yell." She wiggled her fingers at him and Beefy and moved off to sit with her girlfriends.

Webber watched her go, her dark hair swinging like a silky curtain over her fuzzy pink sweater. He turned to grin at Beefy sitting across the table.

"Hey," Beefy said, half-rising. "I just thought of something I need. Call her back."

"Shut up, you animal," Webb said. "She was talking to me."

Beefy shook his head. "I don't get it, Spider Webb. You get in a small accident, have a puny break in your puny leg, and beautiful women start falling all over you, rushing to open doors, bring you food, panting for your puny body."

"Eat your heart out," Webb said, biting into the cake. It was true, he thought, waving at Jan Robb across the cafeteria. Having a broken leg attracted more attention from girls than running the sixteen hundred in record-breaking time. The only girl in the whole school who appeared unimpressed was Dylis Clark. In English, when someone tried to hand her the marker to sign his cast, she'd just stuck her nose in a book.

At the end of the day Webb was wiped out. Beefy was pushing him in the wheelchair past Dylis's locker, where she was taping a Save the Dolphins poster on the outside of the door. She dropped her roll of tape and it landed in the path of the wheelchair. Webb leaned over and scooped it up. He held it out to her.

Dylis stared at him. Her mother had died of cancer about the same time Webb had lost his father. Maybe that was why she dressed in rumpled blouses and skirts that did nothing for her lumpy figure. And her hair stuck out around her face like a lampshade. She took the tape, but she didn't turn back to her locker.

"Taffy Putnam is a friend of mine," she said heavily.

Webb caught his breath. "R-Really?"

She nodded.

Webb wanted to say something, but he didn't know what to say. He always felt uncomfortable around Dylis. In the third grade, after both of them had lost a parent, Dylis cried a lot. The teacher would say something, anything, and Dylis would put her head down on her desk and sob until her body shook. But Webb never cried. When that sharp pang would come, he'd poke someone next to him or make a paper airplane and throw it from the back of the room. One day a father came to their classroom to talk about bike safety. And he had a voice like Webb's father. Webb listened to him and almost stopped breathing. He missed his father so much then that he couldn't keep from crying. He tried staring out the window and rapping his pencil on his desk, but he couldn't stop. It was Dylis who looked back and saw him. She got out of her seat and came back to his desk and put her arms around him. Webb pushed her away and yelled, "Leave me alone!" After that they pretty much ignored each other. To Webb it had always seemed that Dylis Clark lived in a little black cloud, waiting for the end of the world. Maybe she was a poor, broken-up kid, but Webb sure wasn't.

"Well," he said. The name Taffy Putnam roared in his ears. "I'm sorry about . . . I mean, it's really . . . really terrible." He rubbed his hands on his jeans. "Well, I guess I'll see ya, Dylis." He gave her a little wave.

"Geez," Beefy said as they passed through the double

doors on their way to the parking lot. "They must have served dolphin in the cafeteria today."

Webb laughed, but he felt a hard pain in his stomach like Dylis had socked him. Was it true that Dylis knew Taffy Putnam? He guessed that would put Dylis in a black mood. But she didn't have to take it out on him. "She should go jump in the lake with all her dolphin buddies." He slid into the backseat while Beefy loaded his wheelchair.

Webb was so exhausted, he closed his eyes and fell asleep before they were out of the lot. He woke with a start, at some image hanging there in front of him. A small thing with big eyes. What was it? A kitten? Its eyes were wide open, looking straight at him. Terrified.

" 'Lay it down, oh, lay it down,/put it with forgotten things-s-s. . . .' " Beefy was singing with the song on the radio. " 'It will rise, oh, it will ri-i-i-se. . . .' "

"Hey!" Webb yelled, rising out of his sleep.

"Huh?" Beefy turned down the radio. "What's wrong?"

Webb sat forward. "No. Turn it up, turn it up!"

But it was too late—the song was over. Webb closed his eyes again, trying to bring back the image of whatever it was. And the feelings. He couldn't remember. But he felt sick to his stomach. And scared right down to his toes.

chapter 6

WEBB WAS in his room, doing pull-ups on the bar Grampa had installed over his bed.

"Seventy-two, seventy-three," Grampa counted. He was sitting on a chair in the corner, holding the sheet of exercises the therapist had sent home. "Attaboy. You'll be in better shape than you were in October."

Webb let go of the bar and flopped back to the bed. He waited till he had stopped panting before he answered. "Enough upper body. I need leg work," he said.

"So . . ." Grampa peered at the paper. "We work with the weights. Get that left leg in shape. Plenty of time to work on your bum leg after the cast comes off. Another month, you get that off, start working out at

the clinic, and you're good as new. Better than new."
He stood up, picked up the black ankle weight from the
dresser and Velcroed it around Webb's left ankle.
"You'll come back, Boomer. You'll put this town on
the map. About thirty of these to start."

"Fifty. I can do fifty."

"Attaboy." Grampa counted as Webb lifted his leg.
"Three. Think you won't be as fast as you were? I broke
my arm once." He held up his right arm and made a
muscle, invisible under his starched white shirt. "I lifted
cans in the grocery store to get my strength back. Soup
cans, coffee cans, then bigger cans—lard, industrial-size
mustard. Now this is my strongest arm. Where are we?
Nine, ten . . . It works that way—you get stronger in
the broken places. Ernest Hemingway said that somewhere. He was talking about broken arms, broken
legs. Good writer, smart man." He tapped his forehead.
"I'm seventy-five years old. I know about these things.
Someday you'll be glad you broke that leg. Nineteen,
twenty . . ."

Webb groaned. "I may be only fifteen, but I'm not a
total idiot." He gritted his teeth and raised his left leg
again. Would he ever be able to do the same with his
other leg? When he got to fifty, he heaved a sigh.
"What time is it?"

"Six-thirty. Come on, we still got the flexions to
do."

"Beefy's picking me up in thirty minutes. I gotta
shower."

58

"I don't know why you want to go to this party. What can you do? Stand around on one leg and watch people dance? Like watching paint dry. *The Alamo* is on tonight. I love that movie. Boy, you couldn't get me outa the house tonight. John Wayne when he comes into town with all his rough riders . . ." Grampa looked up as if he saw the scene on the bedroom ceiling. "Waiting for the reinforcements that never come. 'There's right and there's wrong,' he says. Remember this, Boomer? 'You gotta do one or the other. You do one and you're living; you do the other and you may be walking around, but you're dead as a beaver hat.' Hah! Dead as a beaver hat." Grampa smiled and stroked his beard. "When Ches gets home, she'll make us some caramel corn. Now that's what I call a good time." He turned back to Webb, his good eye full of hope.

Webb sat up and undid the ankle weight. He had spent the last month going to school and then coming home and falling into bed. After his nap he'd do exercises or try to get a little homework done and then fall back into bed for the night. And he wasn't sleeping that well. Day after day Grampa talked about Taffy Putnam. "She can't eat," he would say, his face defeated-looking. "She can barely move."

And now Taffy Putnam was beginning to haunt Webb's dreams. It wasn't her face—he didn't even know what she looked like. It wasn't even her exactly—this ten-year-old kid on a bicycle that Grampa talked about. It was just waking up and having the sense that something was hurt. A bird with a broken wing, a deer staggering through the woods with an arrow through its side. Once, it seemed like he woke up because he had knocked his mother's favorite bowl off the counter and the fragments of glass screamed like a thousand voices. But when he opened his eyes he was still in the dream and he saw that it was Taffy Putnam screaming. Screaming like he had never heard a little girl scream before. It scared him that something so terrible could happen to a little girl. After a few of these dreams, Webb remembered how, when his grandma was alive, if she saw someone in a wheelchair or with a white cane or even if an ambulance was passing, she would always say, "Bless the broken." Sometimes when he dreamed about Taffy he said that. He figured she could use a sort of a prayer.

Mostly, though, he wished he could stop thinking about her. Every time he heard her name it affected him the way it had when Dylis said it at school. A hard pain in his stomach, like a punch, took his breath away.

He wanted to feel the way he did before the accident. He wanted to go out and have fun with his friends and not think about what had happened and not have strange dreams. He looked up at Grampa and tried to sound lighthearted. "The women are after me. I gotta get back in circulation."

"Aw, bull." Grampa had made a tube of the exercise sheet and cracked it across his hand. "You don't need to be thinking about girls. When I was your age, I had my fun with the guys. Get up a little poker, my mother'd make us a bunch of beef sandwiches."

Webb groaned. "Beefy's playing for this party. So are Wren, Jeff, and the other guys." He slid off the bed and reached for his crutches. "I just want to get out of here, have a little fun for a change."

"You know"—Grampa pointed the paper tube at him—"your father wasn't much of a partyer. He didn't start with that stuff till he went to college."

Webb clenched his teeth, his face heating with anger. "Dammit," he snarled, "I'm not Dad. I'll never play ball. I like to party. Knock it off, will you?" Webb knew Grampa was going through a hard time too, but he was tired of his gloominess. He wanted to listen to music, have a few laughs. He grabbed his crutches and left the room. When Beefy came Webb was waiting out on the front porch, where the first snow of the season was beginning to fall. He left without eating dinner. He didn't even say goodbye to Grampa.

The party was a sixteenth-birthday party for twins— Holly and Molly Ward. They were a year ahead of Webb in school, but he had gotten to know them from his summer job at the marina. They kept their twenty-seven-foot Sea Ray there and waterskied almost every day. When Webb hobbled in behind Beefy and his drums, both twins broke away from the kids in the kitchen and threw their arms around him. "Webbie!"

"Happy birthday," Webb said, grinning sheepishly. "I didn't bring you a present."

"You are the present, hunko," Holly said. She was identical to her sister, tall and skinny, with shaggy brown hair—except that she had dyed the hair around her face orange. "Here," Holly said, shoving some potato chips in his mouth. "We need to fatten you up." She took his crutches and handed them to Beefy. "Carry these downstairs."

"What am I—a packhorse?" Beefy protested. He pointed at his trap case full of snare drum and cymbals.

"Stay in front of him," Molly said. "So he can break his fall with something big and soft. Just in case."

"Geez oh Pete," Beefy complained, lifting the crutches over his shoulder. "You're more trouble than my two-year-old brother."

But Webb was looking down the steep stairs. At school he took the freight elevator, and the only steps he had to negotiate were the few steps at the front of the school building and those of his front porch. Besides being steep, the wooden steps were clogged with kids coming up and going down. He inched over to the banister and took hold. "Just wait a sec till the traffic clears," he said to Beefy.

"Hey!" Holly yelled from behind Webb. "Clear the decks, you guys. We got a handicapped person coming down."

He gripped both banisters and, holding his cast out in

front, he slowly hopped, one step at a time, down the stairs. When he hit the bottom, everyone in the basement started cheering and clapping. Kids were slapping him on the back like he had just broken the sixteen-hundred-meter record.

He grinned and held up his hand, feigning modesty. "Please," he said, "it was nothing."

Beefy groaned as he handed the crutches back. "Why don't we just set up your chair in the center of the room and people can take turns waiting on you?"

Just then Maxie Gallagher and another girl came up. "Hi, guys," Maxie said. She held out a can of pop. "Here, I brought you—"

"Gee, thanks, Maxie." Beefy took the can. "How'd you know I was parched?"

"Beefy!" She snatched it away from him and handed it to Webb.

"You should be ashamed of yourself, Beefy," Webb said, "taking advantage of the infirm." He grinned at Maxie. "Thanks. I really worked up a sweat coming down those stairs."

"Excuse me," Beefy said. "I'm going to puke." He headed upstairs for his trap case.

Webb and Maxie and the other girl stood and watched Dark Secret; the band wore the matching black shirts Webb's mother had made. When they turned around, you could see a big pair of red lips with a woman's finger held up in front. His mother had appliquéd the logo over the left side of the chest. Jeff Scott was tuning his bass. He looked up. "Hey, Spider Webb, how's the leg?"

"Good as new," Webb said, lifting his cast a few inches from the floor. "Almost."

Maxie laughed. "I don't know how you can always be so cheerful," she said. "I broke my finger when I was seven." She held it up and wiggled it back and forth. "It was in a splint for three weeks, and I couldn't stand it. I couldn't comb my hair or write or play the piano or dial the phone or anything." She smiled at him. "You never complain."

Webb laughed wryly. "Well, you should check that out with my grandfather."

"His grandfather," Maxie said to the girl next to her, "is the reason he's got the broken leg. If it was me," she turned back to Webb, "I'd be complaining to him too. After all, he's walking around good as new and here you are—"

"No," Webb interrupted. "I didn't mean that. I don't really blame him or anything."

"See," Maxie said to the girl. "He's just too sweet, isn't he?"

Webb felt a stab of regret for the way he had yelled at Grampa. He started to say something, but he stopped and shrugged. "You're right," he said. "I'm just too adorable for words."

Maxie laughed. Then she and her friend started to sing along when Dark Secret began their first song, "A

Sparrow Frozen in the Snow." " 'It's a hard winter, the winter of the lonely hear-r-rt,' " they sang. Just then two boys pulled them both onto the dance floor. "Bye," Maxie called to Webb over Bob Lyons's shoulder.

Webb watched them for a few minutes, sipping his pop. Maxie's long hair spun out like colored ribbons under the red and green twinkle lights overhead. She had all the moves, Webb thought, as she rocked in perfect time to the music. He imagined he was out there, shaking his body two inches away from Maxie Gallagher's. Then someone dancing by said, "Hey, Webb, you're like a big post in the middle of the floor." His face got warm, and he leaned into his crutches and moved away, looking around the big room. The dance floor was polished wood but beyond that was a thick carpet. How comfortable it would be to lie down on it and take a nap. He shook his head, trying to come alive. The party had only been going for an hour and he was already exhausted. Looking over at the table of food, he realized he was starving. He had skipped dinner.

Holly, Molly, and a bunch of kids were standing around the table, scooping up nachos dripping with cheese. Webb could see a dish full of something like meatballs, another piled with chicken wings. Cheese balls and crackers, bowls of nuts, the usual vegetable tray, some kind of little breads with red stuff on top. Cookies. A big birthday cake. He hesitated, looking for an opening. His head hurt, and he thought about just packing it in for the night. Webb glanced back at Beefy, but he was totally engrossed in the band. No chance for a ride home for quite a while. "Oink, oink," he said halfheartedly.

"Webb!" Molly yelled when she spotted him. "Get out of the way, you guys. Webb wants to eat. Leslie, take this bowl upstairs and tell my mom we need more nachos." She held out a plate to Webb. "Here."

"I think I'll just sidle up to the trough." Webb nodded at the table.

"Molly, don't be so bossy," Leslie said. "And besides, I'm going to stay here and help Webb. How do you think he's going to hold on to a plate of food?" She took the plate from Molly and dumped some meatballs in the center.

"Here." Holly reached across the table and dropped some stuffed mushrooms on his plate. " 'Scuse my fingers."

"Some of these?" Leslie pointed at the chicken wings, and Webb nodded.

Leslie piled some little sandwiches on his plate. "You don't want any vegetables, do you?"

Within a few minutes Webb was seated in a leather chair, his cast stretched out on an ottoman, wolfing down a heaping plate of food, with another loaded plate beside him. Leslie sat on the ottoman, and Holly and Molly sat on the floor on either side of his chair.

"But doesn't your grandfather feel just terrible about

that little girl?" Holly was asking. "I mean, I read in the paper, she might never be normal again. She might be like a, you know . . ." She pointed at a piece of celery.

Webb swallowed. He stopped eating for a second and leaned back into the chair and took a few deep breaths. He was feeling better now that he was sitting down with food in his stomach. His headache had scaled down to a faint throb that sort of kept time to the music. "Yeah," he said, not really wanting to talk about Taffy Putnam, "he does." Then he glanced over at the other end of the room. Maxie was dancing with Peter Pocknis. He had his chin on her head in that irritating way that he did with every girl he danced with. Like he owned her.

"I'll bet you do too," Leslie said, looking at him through her big round glasses. "You must think about it all the time. Go over all the details of the accident a hundred times a day."

Webb shrugged. "I can't remember anything. One minute I'm running down the sidewalk on my way home from school. The next minute I wake up in the hospital."

"Oh, that's really fascinating," Holly said, rolling her eyes. "My aunt's bladder suspension was more interesting."

He smiled, but he was thinking about Maxie. "Excuse me," he said, reaching for his crutches. He negotiated around the ottoman and headed for the dance floor. Threading his way through the couples, he stopped beside Peter and looked into Maxie's face.

"Would you like to dance?"

She grinned at him. "What?"

"I said—"

"Hey!" Peter turned Maxie around so he was facing Webb. "You're blocking traffic, Freegy."

"I'm cutting in," Webb said. Now that he couldn't see Maxie's face, he was beginning to feel a little foolish.

"Go break a leg," Peter said. "I mean another leg."

But suddenly Maxie was standing beside him, laughing. "Sure, I'd love to dance with you. Hold his crutches, would you, Peter?"

"Geez." Peter just shook his head and walked away.

Maxie leaned Webb's crutches against the wall and came back and put her arm around his neck. "Ready?" she said.

He nodded and put both arms around her, balancing on one foot. He breathed in the apple fragrance of her hair as she started swaying against him. Suddenly he felt as shaky as a little twig. "Maxie?"

"Hmmm?" She looked up at him.

"I can't do this."

"You can't?" She started laughing. "Well, thanks a lot, Webber. Ask me to dance and then just stand there."

"Sorry," he said, hopping over to the wall and leaning against it to catch his breath.

Maxie followed him and punched him in the shoulder.

"Ow." He pretended to be in pain.

"What did you ask me for then?"

He grinned. "Maybe I just wanted to hug you."

She groaned. "All this time I've been thinking you were suffering and helpless."

"Well, I am suffering," he said, giving her a pathetic look. "Maybe you'd better sit down with me."

She shook her head, but she followed him to the other end of the room, where he dropped into the big chair. He felt worn out.

" 'Put it with forgotten things-s-s-s . . .' " Frankie Vernon sang at the other end of the room.

" 'It will rise, oh, it will rise,' " sang Maxie, sitting on the arm of the chair, " 'like the bird with silver wings-s-s-s. . . .' "

Webb's head started throbbing again as he turned to watch the band. Then everything around him dropped away. It was a bright, sunny day in October and he was out on Midline Road, driving his grandfather's Lincoln. Not another car on the road. Only her. The little girl.

chapter 7

THERE WERE music and sunlight and leaves the color of fire. Wheeling and pumping, throbbing and beating, like a spun top, like a bright top spun by a child's hand. Humming in the sunshine. Webb saw it that way at first—a bright ribbon of color and happiness. It didn't matter where they were going that October day, he and Grampa. They might have been going for burgers, just joyriding, listening to the pulsing beat of the radio, feeling the sun on his cheeks through the window. But then, quick as an arrow it changed. The music became the sound of glass breaking. From out of the brightness came the pale, frightened face of Taffy Putnam, her wild eyes searching his own. Her ghostlike face rushed at him. He clutched the steering wheel like a life preserver. Again and again, she came at him, telling him in her wordless horror: He was the reason.

Someone was yelling his name.

He lifted his head from his hands and looked around like someone waking from a dream. The kids around him were no longer laughing. They were staring at him.

"What?" He realized the band had stopped—the room was silent. He saw the look on Maxie's face and realized they all must know too. He looked around for his crutches. "I gotta get out of here." He half-rose.

"Now, just take it easy, young man." Mrs. Ward was standing in front of him and pushed him back into the chair. "You'd better sit there and collect yourself for a few minutes."

"I never heard anyone scream like that in my life," Maxie said, laughing nervously.

Webb looked at her. Then at Mrs. Ward, the faces around him. "Sorry," he muttered.

"From the accident," someone said. "Probably the concussion screwed him up."

"Where does it hurt?" Mrs. Ward peered into his face, so close he could smell coffee on her breath. "Is that why you screamed?" She took a glass of water from someone and held it to his lips.

He shook his head and closed his eyes again. Now he felt another wave of memory, just as vivid as the first—tumbling inside the car like a sock inside a dryer, his head striking metal over and over. The fall down a deep and cold well, the final jackhammer blows smashing his

71

leg, the back of his head, the pain ripping apart his bones. The pain was everywhere, in his bones, in every cell of his body, in his heart. "Oh, God," he breathed. He buried his face in his hands and moaned.

Mrs. Ward stood. "I'm going to call your mother."

Webb caught his breath. "Don't." He didn't know what had happened tonight but he didn't want his mother involved. "No," he said more gently. "She—she isn't home tonight. Neither is my grandfather. I just . . ." He groaned, trying to think. "Could you just . . ." He looked away from Mrs. Ward to the faces around him. Kids talking about him. There was Beefy in his black shirt with the red lips, eating a plate of nachos. "Beefy."

"Yeah, I'll take you home," Beefy said, wiping his hands on his shirt. "It's break time anyhow."

Webb nodded and stood up. It took all the energy he had to get back up the stairs and out the door.

Beefy helped him into the backseat and started the car. "Geez," he said, backing down the drive. "Look at it snow. Too bad it's not a school day tomorrow. They'd probably cancel."

Webb stared at the back of Beefy's head as they passed under the streetlights. Beefy's shaggy hair was messier than usual from all the head shaking he did when he played the drums. Webb wished he could see Beefy's face. The round button eyes, the wide surprised lips would tell him what he wanted to know. "Yeah," he murmured, wondering if Beefy was really thinking about snow. Webb sank back against the armrest and looked out the window. He tried to care if he ever went to school again. After a minute he lifted his head. "Beefy?"

Beefy was eating a piece of cake. "Mmuh?"

"Hey, Beefy, what'd I say back there?" He tried to sound lighthearted.

"Say?" Beefy turned the corner, and the old Buick fishtailed on the snowy road. "You didn't say a thing. You screamed like a banshee."

Webb pressed his fingertips between his eyebrows where his head continued to throb. "So—so you don't think I did anything really weird or anything?"

Beefy laughed. "Where I come from yelling is pretty standard behavior. In my family, you run out of hot water, you scream. You can't find your socks, you scream. I don't know why you hollered, but I figure you had your reasons." He shrugged. "Didn't bother me."

Webb blew out a long breath. "Is there anything else?"

"Is there anything else?" Beefy snorted. "You sound like a shrink. Here, have some cake." He offered a crumbling piece of cake over the backseat. "Good for what ails you."

There was no food in the world that was good for what ailed him, Webb thought when he got inside his house. He stood there leaning against the door till Beefy pulled out of his drive. Then he started down the hall to Grampa's room.

The door was open and Grampa was sitting up in bed, sleeping, with his glasses on. On the TV John Wayne stood under a big shade tree, talking to a lady in a long, fancy dress. Webb put his hand on the knob to turn it off, then changed his mind. He didn't want his mother to hear them talking. He shut the door and moved over to the bed. "Grampa," he said, jiggling his arm.

"What—" Grampa shot forward, hands raised as if warding off blows. "Aaah, Boomer." He relaxed and sank back to his pillow. "You came back to watch the movie after all." He pushed up his glasses and squinted at the screen.

"Grampa."

Grampa looked at Webb, his silver hair sticking out at all angles. "Whatsa matter? Hey, you forgot to eat your dinner. There's half a pot of—"

Webb groaned and slumped down in the ladder-back chair in the corner. He lifted his cast and rested it on the foot of the bed. "I know about the accident. I know what happened," he said, his voice breaking.

"What are you talking about—you know? Of course you know. We all know."

Webb ignored him. "I was driving. I remember everything. I was the one who hit that little girl, not you. I sent her to the hospital, I broke your ribs. I did this."

He slapped his cast. Saying it out loud took his breath away. He felt his heart pounding in his chest.

Grampa threw his head back and started laughing. "What—are you crazy? That accident scrambled your brains. You're a nutcase, Boomer." He started laughing again.

Webb watched him, and in the deep pit of his misery he felt a little rising of hope. Maybe he *was* crazy. Could he have imagined that he was driving that afternoon? "It all came back to me at the party tonight," he whispered.

"What?" Grampa, still smiling, motioned with his hand for Webb to go on. "What came back? Tell all."

Webb took a deep breath. "That you . . ." He swallowed and took another breath. Going back to the memory was like stepping into a hail of bullets. He closed his eyes and described what he saw there. "You let me drive and . . ." He cleared his throat and swallowed several more times. "I drove on Midline Road past the cows and the wheat fields and everything was okay. And then." He paused, his heart dropping. "I—I saw this little girl right in front of me. And I couldn't . . ." He cracked his knuckles and took a deep breath. "I hit her." His voice was trembling. "And I remember the rest of it too. Tipping over, the windows breaking." He exhaled. "Everything."

Grampa looked at him. "So you remember?"

Webb nodded.

Grampa sat straight up and pointed at him. "Like you

remember the bricks dropping on your head? Like you remember you and me falling out of the Ferris wheel?"

Webb paused. "That was different." He looked at his grandfather, and he felt the small stirring of hope again. "I think this was different," he said weakly.

"Naw." His grandfather waved the whole thing away. "This is nonsense, Boomer. Were you drinking at this party? Is that it?"

Webb shook his head. "Are you lying to me, Grampa? Because if you are, I want to know. I can handle it," he said, but his voice sounded feeble even to him.

"You can handle it? Okay, Mr. Tough Guy. Here it is. I was driving." Grampa thumped his chest. "I hit the little girl. I'm the one who gets sued. I'm the one who goes to jail. Feel better?"

Webb did feel better but not much. He had been so certain of the memory at the party. It had been as real as life. Now, it seemed, it was just another hallucination. But why was it so powerful? Why did it make him stop breathing when he thought of it?

"Aw, go to bed, Boomer. Turn off the TV."

Webb stood up, nodded, and turned off the television. He moved slowly to the door, aware that his head was pounding again. But it was all right, he thought. This would all be gone in the morning.

At the door Grampa said, "Boomer?"

He turned.

"Do you think, even if you were guilty, I would let you take the blame?"

Webb's heart stopped. He turned all the way around and looked at his grandfather lying there in his rumpled black pants and white shirt, his face so full of love it almost hurt to see. Then Webb knew. Of course his grandfather would lie for him, take the blame for him, go to jail for him. He had just said he would do it. And that was what he was doing. His words were like a knife turning in Webb's heart. He wanted to erase the words, walk out the door, forget everything about this night. But now he could never forget. Now that he knew the truth. He stared at his grandfather. "Why?" he croaked.

Grampa tugged at his beard. "Why what?"

"Why did you do this? Why did you lie about the accident?" Webb's voice was shaking.

Grampa looked at Webb. He answered, his voice brimming with emotion. "You know why, Boomer. Because I love you. I love you more than anything in this life. Because I couldn't stand for you to be hurt over this."

"But Grampa"—Webb lifted his hands in a gesture of helplessness—"didn't you think about this? That I might remember what really happened?" He shook his head. "This changes everything."

Grampa swung his legs over the side of the bed and stood up, grasping Webb by the shoulders. "No, Boomer, don't say that. Don't you see? This changes nothing. Nothing. It's just between us. Nobody else has to know. Your mother, your friends, nobody. I did this. That's the way it'll go down in history. There's no way anyone is going to pin this on you. You're innocent."

Webb looked at Grampa in amazement. "Innocent? What are you talking about? I was the one driving. I'm about as innocent as Adolf Hitler. My conscience will never be clear again. Geez, Grampa." He plowed both hands through his hair and shook his head.

"Now, listen." Grampa poked his finger into Webb's chest. "You have to stop thinking that way. You *are* innocent. There's no guilt attached to you in any way. You were driving only because I let you drive. I knew you were underage, so that makes me responsible. All the blame, all of it, is mine." He thumped his own chest.

"But—"

"Webber, Webber, you're fifteen years old. You have your whole life ahead of you. Do you want this black cloud following you wherever you go? A criminal record, people whispering behind your back. And what's more . . ." He paused to catch his breath. He was wheezing as he always did when he talked too much. "You'll never get a license with this on your record. You can just throw away any notions of picking up your girlfriend for the prom. You will never drive again," he said slowly.

"Oh, God." Webb pressed the heels of his hands

against his eyes. "Grampa," he said in a smothered voice. "I don't know what to do."

"Forget it," Grampa said. "Don't do anything. Just let me take care of everything. I'll always take care of you. You know that."

Webb pressed his hands harder against his eyes. But it didn't do any good. The tears started down his cheeks.

chapter 8

WEBB OPENED his eyes and the first thing he saw was the snow. Flakes the size of potato chips tumbled past his window. He pulled himself up on the overhead bar to look out at the churning, gray lake, and, like a scene from a movie, the window filled with the face of Taffy Putnam. He groaned, letting go of the bar and covering his eyes. In the short hours of the night he had forgotten what had happened, and now it came back, like a sucker punch. He had run over that little girl. She was all broken up in some hospital because of him. Everything, everything had changed. When he'd thought Grampa had done it, he'd felt bad for her, terrible for her. But now he felt sick, hopeless, to think he had ruined somebody's life. And he was scared. More scared than he had been in all his life.

Webb thought back to the day he ran the sixteen hundred, faster than he had ever run it before, how perfect his life had been that afternoon, running down the sidewalk in the sunshine, feeling like anything was possible. He could break the school record, win the state championship. Like Grampa said, he could even run the four-minute mile before he was twenty. Grampa, he thought again. If only Grampa hadn't come looking for him in the car. Or if Webb had turned the corner thirty seconds earlier, they would have missed each other that day. Or, he thought frantically, if only Grampa hadn't let him drive. Grampa should have known better, letting a fifteen-year-old, with practically no experience, get behind the wheel. Even though there wasn't much traffic on Midline Road, that didn't mean there weren't dangers—people walking, riding their bikes. No, he thought, don't think about that part.

Sweat broke out on his forehead when his mind edged into the memory of the accident. He brought his thoughts back to Grampa. If only Grampa hadn't always let him have his way, he thought, a wave of anger washing over him. "Absolutely not," he should have said when Webb asked to drive. "A car is not a toy, Webber." Webb snorted. It was so unlike anything Grampa had ever said to him. But if he had, Webb thought. If only he had. Webb wouldn't be lying there with a broken leg, knowing he had ruined somebody else's life. "God!" Why had Webb even wanted to drive? What a jerk he was, showing off behind the wheel, pretending he was in charge of the world.

"Craphead jerk!" Webb leaned over the bed and grabbed a tennis shoe and heaved it against the white wall, where it left a dirty streak. The vibration knocked over a picture on the nightstand. He was so angry he was panting. He lay back in bed and stared at the ceiling until his breathing returned to normal; then he reached over and picked up the picture that had fallen. It was a snapshot of his father sitting on the front porch, wearing a black-and-red plaid jacket and jeans. He was looking at Webb. Webb had taken the picture one month before his father died. They had been waiting for the pizza man and Webb had run inside for the camera. His father had told him how to hold it, where to press down. Had made the pizza man wait until Webb got the shot. His father was still looking at him. Webb looked away, wanting to pull the covers over his head. He squeezed his eyes shut. What did his father think now?

There was a knock on his door, and his mother stuck her head in. She had silver clips all over her head, holding curls in place until they dried. "You awake?"

He nodded and set the picture back on his nightstand.

She came in and handed him a cup of hot chocolate, then sat down on his bed, her face serious.

Webb caught his breath. His mother knew. Grampa must have spilled the whole story as soon as he got up. "Anything wrong?" He took a sip of hot chocolate, trying to breathe normally.

"Honey, that's what I was going to ask you." She took his hand. "I got a phone call at nine this morning from Wanda Gallagher's daughter, Maxine, wanting to know if you were all right."

"Oh." He nodded. "Yeah, I'm all right."

"She said you were sitting there at the party having a good time and suddenly you just screamed."

Webb snorted. It sounded like he was a real fruitcake. "Yeah," he said. "I guess I did." He grinned at her, like it was a joke.

She didn't smile back. "Well," she said, "are you going to tell me why?"

He shrugged. "I don't know why, Mom. I just . . . I was feeling okay one second and talking with everyone and the next, I kinda just . . ." He shook his head. "I just lost it. It was nothing."

"Nothing? It's not nothing, Webb. It could be an effect of the accident." She put her hand across his forehead as if Webb had a fever. "Does your head hurt? Does anything hurt?"

He shook his head, wishing he could just drop the subject. "I think it was . . . like a flashback, you know? Just for a second, I was back there in the car, when we hit the . . ." He stopped. "You know."

"Oh, Webb. The doctor said that might happen."

She smoothed his hair back from his forehead. "How scary. Do you want to talk about it?"

He shook his head again, not looking at her.

"Are you sure? It might be easier for you if you—"

"Just drop it," he said, pushing her hand away and spilling hot chocolate down his T-shirt. The sudden burning against his chest made him look down at the stain. He rubbed at it, making it worse. Neither of them spoke for a minute. He looked out the window at the lake, almost black now under the glowering sky. "Lake's gonna freeze up," he said, trying to sound cheerful. "I'll have to get my ice skates up from the basement." He forced a laugh.

She laughed too. "Okay—as soon as you're ready, I'll go skating with you. That's a promise."

He nodded. They both hated ice-skating. One year Dad gave Mom ice skates for Christmas, and the three of them laced up and went out on the lake after Christmas dinner. It was a blustery, cold day and they were the only ones out on the whole lake. Webb and his mother stumbled along like two-year-olds while his father sailed off like Wayne Gretzky. "Skate faster," he called across the ice. "You'll warm up." Webb and his mother hung on to each other so that when one of them fell down, the other fell down. "Like this," his father said, windmilling his arms and skating a backward circle around them.

His mother picked herself up and pulled Webber up

beside her. "You big show-off!" she yelled, and she wasn't kidding. "You bought me these ice skates just so you could bring me out here and show off. I hate this! I wanted a velvet jacket. Not ice skates." She put her arm around Webb and led him toward the shore. "Webber hates it too."

Webb glanced back at his father and nodded, relieved that his mother had spoken for him.

"Better not go skating," his mother said now. "We don't want any more broken bones. Your father can keep the record in that department."

"I wish I was more like Dad," Webb said.

"No," she said quickly. "Don't wish that, Webb. Your father was too . . . he wasn't careful. You be careful, that's all I ask. Be careful."

Webb sighed. His mother was the only one who didn't go around bragging to everyone about what a big hero her husband was. Half the time she acted like she was still mad at him for risking his life when he had a wife and son at home. "I hate the way Grampa talks about him," Webb said abruptly. "You'd think he was the one who crawled out on the ice and saved that guy. He brags to everyone like he thinks people are going to think he's some kind of hero for being Dad's father."

"Grampa," she said, shaking her head. "He has visions of glory."

"What a suck-up," Webb added.

"Webb!" She looked upset. "What's the matter with

you?" She put her hand under his chin. "Did something happen between you two? He's acting like an old crank this morning."

Webb looked into his mother's eyes and thought that in five minutes he could tell her everything. Just dump the whole story out like a can of garbage. He might be able to breathe again. But if his mother knew, she would make him come clean with everyone—the police, that little girl's family, his friends. God, how would people look at him when they knew he'd mowed down a little girl? When he had no business driving in the first place. He couldn't handle that, people talking about him wherever he went. He felt another surge of anger at Grampa. "What's he got to be so mad about?" he said hotly. "All he does is complain about how his ribs hurt, how he can barely breathe, how the potatoes that he just bought are sprouting eyes. He's like a little old man."

"Webb, this isn't like you. You're being too hard on him. Maybe you're mad because the accident's made you miss cross-country. But believe it or not, this has been harder on him than on you."

Webb snorted.

"No, I mean it." She started removing the hair clips in fast little jerks and dumping them in her lap. "You know how much he loves you, Webb. Sometimes I think he loves you too much. He would go without food for a week to buy you those running shoes you wanted. And this accident—hurting you—he's just kind of shriveled up into himself. He won't even drive up to the 7-Eleven anymore. And, on top of feeling guilty over you, he has to think about Taffy Putnam. If you knew the burden he carries around." She fluffed the curls with her fingers and shook her head. "He calls the hospital all the time. He's obsessed with that little girl. God." She sighed heavily. "I don't know what's going to become of her."

"Don't!" Webb barked. "I don't want to hear about it." He slid over to the other side of the bed and reached for his crutches.

She came around and handed them to him. "All I'm saying is you're feeling a little too sorry for yourself. Spare a little sympathy for Grampa. He's not in the best of health, and this is dragging him down." She went to the door and turned around. "Webb?"

"What?" he answered hotly.

"Be nice."

"I gotta take a shower."

"Do you want some help?"

"No."

When he came out of the bathroom, his mother said cheerily, "There's somebody in the kitchen to see you."

"Who?" He could hear Grampa talking and someone else laughing. At least Grampa was out of his crappy mood, he thought.

"Just go on." She poked him in the back.

It was Maxie sitting at the kitchen table in a bright

red sweater with a snowman on the front. She was smiling up at Grampa, listening to a story Webb had heard a hundred times.

". . . coming home from the grocery store with a sack of sugar for my mother. When I saw the smoke pouring out of the sacristy window—the window that shows St. Sebastian stuck with arrows—I thought, I've got to save the church. So I put the sugar on the sidewalk and ran thirteen blocks, faster than I've ever run before or since, to the fire station. And I said, 'The church is on fire! The church is on fire!' And they let me ride along on the engine to watch them put it out. If it hadn't been for me, old St. Mary's wouldn't be standing in Detroit today. I was six years old, and they gave me a medal for saving the church. I'll bet I can still find that medal. . . ."

Maxie, smiling, looked over at Webb. "Hi. I had to bring a check over for the draperies so"—she shrugged—"I thought I'd see how you were doing."

"I'm fine," he said, quickly tucking his shirt into his jeans.

She looked back at Grampa. "I think you were wonderful to save your church. Wasn't he, Webb?" She smiled at Webb.

She looked so cute sitting there at the kitchen table with a big smile that Webb grinned back. "Yeah," he said. "My grampa's real wonderful." He sat down opposite her, leaning his crutches against the stove.

"Your girlfriend is very pretty. You should bring her around more."

Webb blushed. "She's not . . . ah . . ." He looked at Maxie and shook his head, feeling his ears burning. They both started laughing.

"Sorry, I didn't know you were here. I was in the shower." Webb ran his fingers through his still-damp hair.

"That's okay. Your grampa has been telling me some very interesting things."

Webb glanced at Grampa. "I'll bet," he said heavily. Their eyes met, and Webb felt the burden of last night all over again.

"He told me that you got up at five-thirty every morning this summer to run for an hour and a half before you went to work."

"Even in the rain," Grampa said over his shoulder as he mixed pancake batter.

"Even in the rain," Maxie repeated. "That's dedication."

"That's stupidity," Webb said, shrugging.

"That's not stupidity," Grampa said, turning around with the blue bowl cradled against his stomach. He lifted the wooden spoon out of the batter and pointed it at Maxie. "You ever hear of Roger Bannister?"

She looked at him blankly.

"Broke the four-minute mile in 1954—three fifty-nine point four. That's how he did it too. Getting up and running an hour and a half a day. That's what Webber has, that kind of perseverance. See this?" He reached up in the cupboard for the Wheaties box and set it in front of Maxie. "In a few years you'll be looking at Webber's face on this box. Coach Brewer called here after the accident. Says to me, 'I don't know what we'll do without your boy. They just don't come a dime a dozen—runners with heart.'" He looked at Maxie, pointing at his heart. "That's what he's got. Our boy's got heart."

"Oh, I love heart," Maxie said, smiling at Webb.

Under Maxie's admiring gaze, Webb's spirits lifted. He picked up an orange, threw it in the air, and caught it. He did it again and smiled at Maxie.

Grampa put the spoon back in the bowl and clapped a hand on Webb's shoulder. "This boy means everything to me, Mary."

"Maxie," Webb said, carefully not looking at Grampa. "Her name is Maxie. She doesn't want to hear about that."

"Yes I do," she said, smiling up at Grampa. "I think it's wonderful that you both love each other so much."

"We do," Grampa said. He turned off the burners under the griddle and turned back to Maxie. "Let me tell you, it's a rare thing when a grandfather loves his grandson more than he loves himself."

Webb exhaled loudly and looked at the ceiling. Grampa was pretending that everything was perfect, that they were just a jolly grandfather and grandson. He had to get Maxie out of the kitchen, away from Grampa. He wondered if she liked walking in the snow. She had walked over here, hadn't she?

Then Grampa said it. "I had a son once—" He closed his eyes and touched his heart.

"Don't start that!" Webb jumped up and leaned on the table, suddenly furious that Grampa was going to try and dazzle Maxie with his father's death.

"I'm only—"

"Shut up!" Webb yelled. "Why can't you just keep your big mouth shut?" He grabbed his crutches, knocking over a chair, and stormed out of the kitchen.

He went out the front door and took a deep breath of the frosty air. He put his hand on the icy railing and squeezed it so hard he could feel the grains of rust grinding into his palm. "What a bunch of crap," he said, closing his eyes.

Behind him, the door opened. It was Maxie. She was holding his letter jacket. "I thought you might be cold," she said shyly.

He took the jacket. "Sorry," he said. "About that." He nodded in the direction of the house.

"Are you still mad?"

Webb looked at the little puffs of air coming out of Maxie's mouth when she talked. He shook his head and zipped up his jacket.

"I get mad at my parents too—all the time. Especially my dad. You should hear how he nags me. 'You have too much lipstick on,' 'You spend too much time on the phone,' blah, blah, blah.'' Maxie slapped the railing with her red mittens as she talked. "Sometimes I wish he'd just disappear."

Webb didn't say anything.

"Oh, my God." She clapped her hand over her mouth. "I'm sorry. I'm so sorry."

Webb shook his head. "Hey, that's okay." She looked so embarrassed he felt sorry for her.

"I keep forgetting about your father. I mean, I don't really forget, but when I'm with you, you seem so normal and everything that you don't seem like somebody whose father died, whose father was this huge hero. Like anyone could really forget that."

"I want you to forget it," he said, turning to look at her. Her cheeks were bright red, and he didn't know if it was from the cold or because she was embarrassed. He wanted to take her hand and say, "Let's walk in the snow." Instead he said, "I'm just me."

She smiled. "You're so sweet." She lifted her face and kissed him on the cheek. Before he could say anything, she hurried down the steps and out to the street. At the corner she turned to wave.

chapter 9

AFTER THE terrible weekend, Webb had to deal with going back to school and facing all the kids from the party. Holly came flying down the hall as he was going into homeroom. "Webbie!" she screeched. "Are you okay? I worried about you all weekend."

"Yeah," he said, glancing around uncomfortably.

She clutched his arm dramatically. "What was wrong?" she demanded. "Why did you scream like that?"

Webb was conscious of people looking at them, stopping in the hall to hear what he would say. He cleared his throat. "Holly," he said soberly, "you know that"— he paused to look around—"that birthday cake? Just what did your mother put in it?"

She looked at him blankly for a second. And then her face broke up. "You big goof!" She slapped him on the arm. "Wait till I tell my mother what you said!"

Webb left her there, laughing as he went into homeroom, relieved that he had gotten away with it. He managed to laugh it off every time someone asked him about the party, but by lunchtime he had run out of steam. He was tired of being funny, tired of trying not to think of Taffy Putnam. And then Peter Pocknis came up with a huge, gloating smile on his face.

"Hey, Webber, I just saw the Warbeck Funny Farm wagon pull up in front of the school. They were looking for you."

Webb ignored him, handed a brownie across the table to Beefy.

"How're you going to man those crutches with a straitjacket on?"

Webb continued to ignore him until Peter rapped him on top of the head with his lunch tray. Webb felt an explosion of anger inside his chest that sent fire all the way down to his toes. His arm flashed up and pushed Peter's tray backward. Then he shoved his chair back so fast he knocked Peter down. Webb got to his feet at the same time Peter did. Holding the table for support, he grabbed Peter by his shirt, which was splattered with spaghetti sauce. "Back off, you clumsy moron."

Peter just stared at him, stunned. Webb collected his crutches from Beefy and hobbled away.

"Can't he even take a little joke?" Peter said to Beefy.

Webb left the cafeteria and started down the hall toward his biology class, changed his mind and turned around. He didn't know where he was going. He crutched down the hall, not conscious of anyone else, of anything at all. His heart was pounding and he was breathing as hard as if he'd just finished a race. He passed all the classrooms in the east wing and came to the end of the building, where there was a single door leading out to the parking lot. He shifted his crutches and put his hand out to push the door bar.

"You can't use that door."

Webb turned to see Dylis Clark standing behind him next to her open locker.

"Buzz off, Dylis," he snarled. "Go save the dolphins." He put his hand out again.

"The alarm will go off," she said.

Webb stopped. He hadn't remembered the alarm. The thought that he couldn't just open the door and go out made him furious. He turned back to Dylis. Her smug, scolding lumpishness summed up everything that conspired to trap him, to keep him from ever being free again. "Would you just get the hell out of my way, Clark? Would you just take yourself into orbit?" He planted his crutches in the direction he had just come.

She snorted. "I'm not in your way, Webber. You're in your own stupid way. Everyone knows you can't use that door."

Webb glared at her.

Just then the freight elevator opened and the janitor got off, pushing a dolly loaded with boxes between them. Webb turned away from Dylis, his heart pounding. He got on the elevator without looking back, hit the "B" button, and the doors closed. When he got out he was barely conscious that he was in the school basement. Big cardboard boxes lined the opposite wall—boxes that said in red letters: CHICKEN NOODLE SOUP, MUSTARD, CHOCOLATE SYRUP. Webb stood there, looking at the boxes, reading the words without knowing what they meant. He looked down the long, gray hallway, at the cement floor, the cinder-block walls, the low ceiling crisscrossed with pipes. He started moving between the walls of boxes. Canned fruit, powdered milk, cleaning products. Where the hallway stopped, he turned right, into the boiler room.

A blast of heat hit him when he approached the huge gray furnace in the middle of the room. It hissed and snarled like a mad dog. Webb circled it once, ducking the thick gray arms overhead. He walked around it several more times, knocking an empty metal bucket out of the way with a thrust of his crutch. The clanging racket made him look quickly around. The last thing he wanted was company. But no one came. Finally he stopped walking. His breathing slowed to almost normal. The feeling that he wanted to break every window in the school dissipated to a general misery. He moved over to a bank of boxes labeled FLOOR CLEANER and sank down, pulling off his backpack and dropping his crutches beside him. With both hands he lifted his cast to a box filled with toilet paper and leaned back, feeling the roughness of the cinder block through his cotton shirt.

Nobody would ever find him down here. He glanced out the door. No one around. As long as big-mouth Dylis didn't report him, he was safe, he thought, remembering how she'd gone straight to the principal when she found out he and Beefy had filled her aluminum-recycling box with leftover pizza from the Fall Fling.

After a few minutes he started wondering what Peter Pocknis was thinking. Probably worrying about how to get the spaghetti stain out of his shirt. That would be the last time that imbecile would get frisky with him, Webb thought, feeling a little better. He sighed and looked around the gray room. If he stayed down here, he'd never have to see Dylis Clark again. Or Pocknis. Or even Grampa. He spotted a huge box of canned peaches against the opposite wall. All he needed was a can opener, he mused. If anyone came down, he could duck behind the boiler. He wondered how long it would be until people forgot about him, stopped looking for him. There'd been a story in the paper the week before about a couple who finally had a memorial service for their daughter after seven years. She had just disappeared from her home one night, drove off in her car, and was never heard from again. They never found her car or her body. Maybe she had driven down to

South America, Webb thought. Maybe she was holed up in Buenos Aires under another name. Making her living leading mountain climbers into the Andes.

He looked around the room once more. There wasn't a window anywhere—just one yellow patch of light from a bulb in the ceiling. How would he get fresh air? And what about running? There was barely room to turn around. It was like a prison cell, he thought, looking slowly around him. Is this what it was like when you committed a murder or robbed a bank? Did they sentence you to a hot little cement room with no windows, no TV, no place to move around? Was that where they sent people who were convicted of negligent homicide?

"Oh, God." Webb put his head in his hands and groaned. He pictured himself shut away like this for ten years, fifteen years, until he was a grown man with a gray beard. All for one little mistake, a few minutes of his life. He'd driven down Midline Road for maybe seven minutes, that was all. There was no one around. How was he to know a little girl would show up out of nowhere? Other little kids took the bus home from school. She shouldn't have been out there all alone. Anything could have happened to her. A dog could have attacked her. She could have slipped on the gravel shoulder and fallen into the path of a car. Maybe that's what happened, he thought desperately. He closed his eyes, trying to see it that way. What he saw was Taffy Putnam on her bike, her face pale as milk, frozen in terror, caught in front of the Lincoln like a wounded bird. He had hit her. Not some drunk driver. Not Grampa. He sat for a long time with his eyes closed, listening to the hiss of the furnace, imagining himself in jail.

"Hey, what are you doing in here?"

Webb looked up. He recognized one of the janitors—a burly, red-faced man with tattooed arms—standing in the doorway.

Webb struggled to his feet. "I . . . ah . . . I left something down here." He reached for his backpack.

"Don't give me that crap. Were you messing with something in here?" The janitor squinted around the room, checking for damage. When Webb crutched to the door, he blocked his way. "I'm going to report you. What's your name?"

"Listen," Webb said, "I wasn't doing anything. I just . . . there was this test I didn't want to take in biology. So I just . . . " He shrugged.

The janitor glared at him for a long moment, breathing his cigarette breath in Webb's face. Finally he stepped aside. "I'll remember you," he said, poking him in the chest. "Mr. Busted Leg."

Webb moved past him and hobbled down the hall, wishing he could run, wishing he could at least walk. He didn't look back, but he could feel the man watching him until he got on the freight elevator. When he got to the first floor, he looked at the clock: 2:15. He had missed biology and part of English. There was no way he was going into English now, having to make up some story about where he'd been the last hour and twenty minutes. If he left the school through the front doors, he'd have to pass the office, where somebody would stop him. "God!" It was like there was somebody up there dropping boulders in his path. He turned to the east-wing door. Sure enough, overhead was a yellow sign: DO NOT USE THIS DOOR AFTER 9 A.M. ALARM WILL SOUND.

Webb took a deep breath and pushed open the door with his rear end, thrusting one crutch out to support himself. At the same time the alarm went off—a loud honking, like a tornado alert. Webb didn't look back. He crutched down the two steps, through the parking lot, and out to Market Street. Let them come after him, he thought. What would they do—make him clean erasers?

It was a cold December day with snowflakes churning through the air. They stung his skin like pinpricks and slipped down inside his cotton shirt. The cold was shocking after being in the boiler room. He was glad of his backpack of books. It was the only protection he had from the chill. Before his broken leg, he had run the three miles to his house in less than twenty minutes. Now it would probably take him an hour, if he didn't freeze to death first, he thought, trying to move faster on the slippery sidewalk. After the first two blocks, he was shivering hard. He stopped and leaned his crutches against a tree and rotated his arms like windmills to get the blood circulating.

"Boomer!"

At first, Webb's heart lifted when he saw Grampa pull up and stop the car beside him. But just as quickly, he dreaded looking into Grampa's face. He grabbed his crutches and started moving down the sidewalk again. But Grampa got out of the car and caught up with him, steering him, talking faster than Webb could think.

"What are you doing, Boomer? Look at you standing out in the snow like a little match girl. And where's your jacket? Why didn't you call me if you needed a ride? The school called me and said there'd been a fight in the lunchroom. You missed your biology class. Nobody knew where you were. I was worried sick. I had to come and find you myself. Here, put this around you—you're freezing." He tucked his black overcoat over Webb in the backseat.

"I thought you were never going to drive again," Webb said through chattering teeth.

"For frivolous things." Grampa looked at him in the rearview mirror as he pulled away from the curb. "This was important. You're frozen like a Popsicle. To save my grandson from freezing to death, I get behind the wheel."

Shut up, Webb wanted to shout. *Stop trying to make me feel grateful.* He slumped back against the seat.

Grampa looked over his shoulder at Webb. "About

the accident," he said gently, "forget it, Webber, just forget the whole conversation." When Webb didn't respond, he went on, "Is that why you're acting so strange, Boomer, getting in fights? Walking around in the snow?"

"Grampa." It came out like a wail. Webb bit his lip and looked out the window so he wouldn't start crying. He made himself concentrate on a gas-station attendant changing the price of gasoline on his sign.

"Maybe you're worried about me," Grampa said. "Because I caused that terrible accident and hit that little girl. You don't know what's going to happen to me. I got the hearing coming up. Maybe you're thinking about that. Hell," he said, raising both hands off the wheel, "could be you're even mad at me. You're hobbling around on crutches for months, missing the whole running season. But I think you should let bygones be bygones, Boomer."

Webb snuffled loudly and gave a bitter laugh. "Don't feed me crap, Grampa. I know what I did. You know what I did. Pretty soon the whole world will know what I did." He wiped his nose on the sleeve of Grampa's coat. "I can't stand it, Grampa. It scares me more than anything to think about what I did—"

"Not what *you* did!" Grampa yelled. He pulled the Lincoln over to the curb. "This is my fault—all of it!" he yelled, looking over the seat. "I never should have let you drive. It was illegal and idiotic and stupid. You got no experience behind the wheel. Something comes up in front of you—how do you know what to do? A fifteen-year-old kid?" When he saw Webb's face, Grampa got out of the car and slammed the door. He opened the rear door and climbed in, grabbing Webb and pulling him against his thin chest. "Baah. I'm such a damn fool. Look what I've done to you. How can I ever forgive myself? You've got to let go of this, Boomer." He squeezed him harder. "Please, please, Webber, let it go. I'm responsible for it, the whole thing. Whatever happened, I did it. Whatever is to come, I'll carry it. Do you hear me, Boomer?" He pulled back and looked at Webb.

Webb looked into his grandfather's eyes, the sad, droopy face. He heard Grampa saying he was to blame for everything. But that didn't change who'd been in the driver's seat, who'd hit the little girl. Webb looked away, his thoughts irresistibly pulled back to that October afternoon.

Grampa shook him. "Webber."

"What?"

"Haven't I always taken care of you, done the very best for you? Made sure you were safe, made sure you were happy?"

Webb nodded.

"Would I ever do anything to hurt you in any way?"

Webb shook his head.

"Trust me," Grampa said. "This is the right way to

go. I'll take care of you. Just let it go." He punched him playfully in the jaw. "Come on, Boom Boom. You trust me, don't you?"

Webb nodded slowly.

Later in the afternoon, Webb got a phone call. He was chopping onions for Grampa's meatloaf, and he wiped his hands on Grampa's apron as he passed him on the way to the hall phone. His spirits lifted when he heard Maxie's voice. Of course, she wanted to know what had happened with Peter.

"I know he's always ripping on you and all that, but what set you off today?"

"Oh, man, I don't know," Webb said, suddenly embarrassed at the scene he had caused in the cafeteria. "Listen, I'm not usually that rough on people."

"No," Maxie said quickly, "it's okay. I mean, he's a jerk. He deserved it." And then she said, "Did you open the door and set off the alarm?"

Webb groaned.

"Are you a rebel or what?" Maxie said, and she started laughing. "I've always had the biggest urge to bust out of that door."

"It was a brilliant maneuver," he said. "I'll probably get ten detentions."

She giggled. "Yeah." Then she said in a more serious voice, "You know something? You're different than I thought you were. When I'd see you in homeroom or in the halls, you always seemed kind of quiet—not exactly shy, but sort of in your own world. And it turns out you're this raging maniac."

Webb snorted. "You like that in a man? Criminal behavior? C'mon over, I'm going to knock off the Kent Bank at seven-thirty."

"Mmmm," she said. "Sounds like fun. Are you serious?"

"About knocking off the bank?"

"No, about coming over."

Maxie, he thought. The one bright spot in his crappy life. "Sure," he said, "that'd be great. My mom will make us some caramel corn." They'd have to put up with Grampa hovering over them. But he didn't even mind. When he hung up the phone, he was grinning at his reflection in the mirror.

chapter 10

WEBB ALMOST forgot about Christmas. Maxie had gone off to Florida with her family the week before, and Webb wasn't too interested in going to the Christmas dance at school. Of course, his mother and Grampa put up a tree, but putting on the ornaments while hopping around on one foot was a bigger chore than trying to take a shower.

The day before Christmas, Webb realized he didn't have a present for his mother and begged a ride from Beefy to K mart. He looked around at the plastic elves hanging from the ceiling, the candy canes, and the tinsel from one end of the store to the other and wished he had enough money to go somewhere nicer. Wandering down one aisle after another, he looked at fruitcake and plastic plants and glittery candles. He stopped at the jewelry counter to look at some gold chains. "How much are these?" he asked the girl behind the counter.

"Seven dollars an inch."

"Um . . ." He only had enough for three inches.

"Do you have anything that looks like that but . . ."

"Cheaper?" She took out another tray of chains that were marked $14.99.

Webb looked at them. They were dull and thick compared to the real gold chains. He wanted to buy his mother something that would really knock her out. She loved pretty things, and there was no one to buy her gold necklaces anymore, or fancy sweaters.

He shook his head. "I guess not."

"These are on sale." She pointed to a display of gold bangle bracelets strung on a plastic tube. "Twenty bucks. Ordinarily thirty-five."

"Each?"

"Well, you just need one. One makes it seem more important."

When Christmas morning arrived, Webb lay in bed and watched the snow drive in a slanted sheet over the lake. It was going to be a cold winter, he guessed, leaning up on his elbows. Already the lake was frozen a couple of inches thick. He wondered if the walleye were biting. That was how he and his father had spent their last Christmas Day together—his father standing over a hole, jigging for walleye, and Webb sliding back and forth on the ice in his rubber boots. They'd had the walleye for Christmas dinner, and he'd felt proud and excited when his mother brought out the baked fish on a silver tray, with mashed potatoes piped all around it like snow. He felt a painful tug at his heart for those days when his father was alive, the uncomplicated joy of Christmas, of walking out on the ice with no sense of dread. He'd rather be out there now, he thought, than under the Christmas tree, pretending to be merry.

From the living room came the strains of "White Christmas." It was his mother's signal, since he was little, that it was time to get up and open presents. He wanted to pull the covers over his head, but he got out of bed, grabbed his crutches, and clumped down the hall to the living room. His mother was sitting beside the tree in her blue robe, waiting for him. She jumped up to hug him. "Merry Christmas, honey."

He kissed her cheek. "Merry Christmas, Mom." When she pulled back he stared at her. "What'd you do to your hair?"

"Oh." She did a quick twirl. "I lightened it. Do you like it?"

"Wow—bright." He put his hand up as if shielding his eyes from a blinding light. Then he said, "It looks nice." His mother was a little sensitive about certain parts of her body. She was pretty, with a nice round face and blue eyes, the same as his, and perfectly straight brown hair, just like his. Her hair tortured her. She thought it was too straight, so she curled it every morning. Or she got it cut or, once in a while, tried a new color.

"Well," she said, patting it self-consciously, "I thought I'd brighten up for the holidays."

Grampa came out of the kitchen with a cup of coffee. He set it on top of the TV and pulled Webb against his chest. "Merry Christmas, Boomer."

Webb hugged him back halfheartedly. "You too," he said, and pulled away.

They sat around the tree and started on the presents. Mom opened hers first—a white chiffon scarf with colored leaves all over it from Grampa and the bracelet from Webb. It wasn't nice enough, Webb thought, watching her try it on and ooh and aah like it was genuine gold. He should have borrowed some more money from Beefy, bought her something really nice. She worked six days a week to take care of them, and Webb wasn't doing a thing to help her.

"This is lovely, Webb," she said, getting up to kiss him.

"I'm coming back to work next month," Webb said. "As soon as I get this off." He slapped the cast. "Then I can afford to buy you something nice."

"Don't be silly, Webb. This is perfect. It goes with my hair." She laughed and went over to kiss Grampa.

Webb looked away while Grampa opened his present, already regretting it. It was a coupon book for ten free pizzas. Beefy's sister, who worked at Arnie's Pizza, had given it to him.

"What's this?" Grampa held up the coupon book.

"Pizza." Webb shrugged. "I guess you don't like pizza that much. Sorry, I was a little strapped for cash." When he was little he always knew that he was giving his mother his school picture in a handmade paper frame and that he would buy his father a crazy-colored fishing lure from his allowance. But Grampa's gift was always a big deal. One year his mother had showed him how to braid leather strips for a key chain that Grampa still carried today. Another Christmas, his dad helped him build a birdhouse and he painted it purple—Grampa's favorite color. Webb looked away from Grampa, embarrassed. "Sorry," he muttered again.

"Well," his mother said, "I never get sick of pizza. I could eat pizza every night for ten nights in a row. Here, honey."

She handed him a present that Webb could tell was a book. Every year she got him a mystery, which was the only kind of book he read outside school. He took off the wrapping. It was about Roger Bannister. He looked at her. "How did you—"

"Grampa suggested it." She reached over and patted Grampa on the knee. "We know how discouraged you've been lately because you miss running, and he thought this book might inspire you. I hope it does, sweetheart."

Webb nodded, annoyed at Grampa. Did he think that

what troubled him could be fixed by reading a book? He forced a smile. "Thanks, Mom."

"I know you're going through a bad time," she went on. "But just think—in another month you'll have no cast at all. This will be just like a bad dream."

Webb had a sudden image of Taffy Putnam, and his face flamed with guilt. He stared at the floor and nodded, not trusting himself to speak.

The last present he opened was from Grampa. It was a pair of Nike Air Max TLs. Webb just sat there staring down at them. If Grampa had only waited, he thought, if he had waited until now instead of trying to get them in October, everything would be different. Webb would be jumping for joy. He would be lacing them up, jogging around the living room, jostling ornaments off the tree. He held them up. "These are great," he said, trying to sound like he meant it.

"Do you like them?" Grampa asked anxiously. "I can't wait to see you wearing them, running around the track, leading the whole pack. Try them on, Boomer."

Their eyes met briefly, and Webb saw how Grampa's eyes were pleading with him to be the happy little eight-year-old, flinging himself headlong into the presents, into the whole charade. Did he expect Webb to run over and throw his arms around him and say that now he had his shoes his happiness was complete? Webb looked away. "Sure," he said. "After breakfast, okay?"

So it was over, and the three of them went out to the kitchen to fix breakfast together, with his mother exclaiming brightly about what a lovely Christmas it was and how much use she would get from her presents. Webb was falsely hearty, feeling worse, somehow, than if he had just sat there sullenly picking at the omelette Grampa had made. He was glad when the phone rang and it was for him.

"Merry Christmas," Maxie said cheerily. "Was Santa Claus good to you?"

"Hey," he said, "are you home?"

"We got home late last night. Do you think I could stop by?" she said. "I have something for you."

"You do?" Webb's heart dropped. He hadn't even thought of getting anything for Maxie. "Sure," he said quickly. "That'd be great." After he hung up, he groaned, "Oh, no."

His mother came out of the kitchen, wiping her hands on a towel. "What are you moaning about?"

"Maxie's coming over with a present for me. Where am I going to get a present for her on Christmas morning? Geez oh Pete, I didn't even think—" He looked around the room desperately at the Christmas tree, the ornaments, the angel on top, the clay vase he had made in the sixth grade with a piece of holly stuck in it.

"Give her this." Grampa came out of the kitchen and pulled the pizza coupons from his sweater pocket.

Webb rolled his eyes. He waved it away.

"Oh, Webb, here." His mother held out the gold bracelet. "We'll put it back in the box and wrap it up."

He looked at her in surprise. "No," he said. "I bought that for you."

"Go on," she insisted, putting it back in its red box. "You can owe me next year."

Maxie exclaimed over the bracelet even more loudly than his mother had. "Oh, Webb, this is gorgeous. You must have spent a fortune on it."

"Well," he said, watching her slip the bracelet over her slender, tanned hand, "we did have to take out a second mortgage on the house." He felt stupid watching her put it on with his mother sitting right there watching too. Maxie had brought his mother a box of saltwater taffy from Florida. And she brought Grampa a giant seashell.

"Is this the kind you can hear the sound of the ocean?" He held it up to his ear.

"Probably the sound of traffic," Maxie said, laughing. She looked great with her tan. "Florida is jammed with cars this time of year."

"This candy looks too good to save," his mother said, jumping up. "You'd all better help me, or I'm going to look like Hilda Hippo by New Year's." She passed the box around. Then she pulled Grampa out of his chair to help her check the turkey.

"Your mom's nice," Maxie said, twirling her hair around her finger. "She's sort of diplomatic, isn't she?"

Webb laughed. "Sort of."

"Here." Maxie handed him a small green foil box. "It's not much," she added as he pulled off the gold bow.

He took off the lid. It was a key chain with an alligator on it. "This is great."

"It's just a souvenir," she said, clasping her hands together, "but I figured you wouldn't have one yet."

He shook his head. "No, I don't. Thanks a lot, Maxie."

His mother came out with hot chocolate and admired the key chain.

"Webb and I will be taking driver training at the same time," Maxie told her, bouncing up and down on the sofa. "In March. My dad is buying me a car for my sixteenth birthday. It's not until July," she said to Webb, "but I can hardly wait. Can you?"

Webb grinned. "Nope. You can pick me up and take me with you to the club pool every day." The Gallaghers belonged to the Lemon Lake Country Club where Webb had never once set foot. He knew she belonged there by the burgundy-colored sweaters and sweatshirts she wore with LLCC in gold across the chest. Besides, she never swam at the beach like the rest of the kids.

Maxie kept on talking. "Do you want to see what else I got? Here." She pulled back her long hair. "I got these earrings from my mother—diamond chips—and this watch from my dad." She rolled back her sweater sleeve to reveal a gold watch on the same wrist as the bracelet. "And this sweater from my brother and . . ."

Webb looked at his mother with a sinking feeling. Her bracelet was just a cheesy souvenir next to all the expensive presents Maxie was wearing. If she felt bad, his mother didn't show it. She examined and praised every gift as if she had received it herself.

"Well, I'd better go," Maxie said. "My mom's doing the turkey thing."

Webb went to the door with her. "Do you want to do something later—maybe go to the movies with Beefy and Monica?"

Maxie gave him a big smile. "I'd way rather do that than watch *It's a Wonderful Life* for the millionth time with my parents."

After Maxie left, his mother picked up the box of candy. "I'm going back in my room and eat the rest of these, and then I'm going to run them off." She made a face. Running on her treadmill was worse punishment than ice-skating. "Call me when dinner's ready."

Webb looked at her in her old blue robe, with her gold hair, and put his arms around her. He could hardly breathe. "Sorry about your bracelet," he murmured.

"Oh, pooh."

"I feel like such a jerk, giving her the bracelet I bought for you. I mean, geez, I should have bought her something."

"Girlfriends have to be maintained," she said, poking

him in the chest. Then she laughed. "You'll get the hang of it." She laughed all the way down the hall to her room.

Webb clumped back into the kitchen, where Grampa was chopping up onions for stuffing. He had a piece of dry bread stuck in his mouth—his formula for keeping his eyes from watering. The turkey sat on the counter all washed and buttered, waiting to be stuffed. The wooden table was loaded with preparations for the dinner—a bag of potatoes, a bag of celery, onions, squash, a can of cranberry sauce.

Grampa took the bread out of his mouth. "Did your girlfriend leave?" he asked, dumping the onions into a metal bowl.

Webb didn't answer. He lowered himself on a stool at the end of the counter, leaned his crutches against the table. "Where do you want me to start?"

Grampa wiped his hands on the Rudolph the Red-Nosed Reindeer apron Webber had given him years ago. He pressed his hands against his chest. "Start here, Webb. Start with me. Talk to me. Smile at me. I'm not a stone. I'm not a—a—" He looked around the kitchen. "I'm not a toaster. I'm a human being. A human being who just happens to love you more than life itself."

Webb shrugged and picked up a potato. He tossed it up and caught it. "I am talking to you. See?"

"I don't understand you, Boomer. Don't understand why you're giving me the cold shoulder. You're acting

116

like I did something to deliberately hurt you. You know I'd cut off my right arm"—he held it out and made a chopping gesture with his other hand—"before I'd do anything to hurt you. Maybe I'm stupid, maybe I'm a stupid old man, but I don't honestly know why you're mad at me, Boomer. Tell me what I did that's so terrible."

Webb studied the potato. Every thought about the accident, about Taffy Putnam, was like a big hand squeezing his heart. Without thinking, he put his hand there and shook his head.

"I know this is about the accident—" Grampa said, and stopped. "Where's your mother?"

"She's in her room," Webb said. He wished his mother would suddenly appear to interrupt them. It had been weeks since they had talked about it, since the day he left school early. Thinking about it terrified him. He hated the way the fear took over his whole body. Now the awful feeling was rushing at him again, filling him with a wild panic. He tried to take a deep breath, unable to speak.

"If you're mad at me for breaking your leg, okay. But—"

"No," Webb croaked.

"The other?"

Webb nodded.

Grampa came over and stood in front of him. Webb could smell the mix of sage and onions on his hands. "Blame me," he said mournfully. "I blame myself. But,

117

Webber, don't hate me. I'd rather be dead than have you hate me."

Webb took another deep breath. He lifted his eyes and looked at his grandfather standing there in the red apron, little crumbs of bread stuck in his beard. "I don't hate you, Grampa."

"Boomer." Grampa flung his arms around Webb.

Webb pulled away. "What difference does it make? Whether I hate you or whether I love you, it doesn't make anything better, does it? It doesn't make that little girl get out of her bed and start jumping up and down for joy, does it?"

"Oh, Boomer," Grampa said, folding him in again. "I've always taken care of you, haven't I? Remember when you had chicken pox—how brokenhearted you were when somebody else got to take home that guinea pig for the summer?"

"God." Webb groaned. "This is not a guinea pig problem, Grampa."

"I know, I know. But back then, when I brought you that guinea pig home in a glass box, you thought I was a hero. I had solved the worst problem in your seven-year-old life with just the snap of my fingers."

"No." Webb shook his head. "That's nothing like this."

"What about your father then? You can't say that wasn't the most terrible experience a young boy could ever go through—losing his father. Your whole world dropped out from under you. Everything you had ever counted on, you could never count on again. At eight years old you had to face the worst that life can dish out, something most of us don't deal with till we're fifty, sixty years old. But you didn't have to face it alone, did you? Oh, I'm not saying I made everything just peachy, that I waved a magic wand and everything was okay for you." Grampa paused again for air, his lung wheezing like an ancient accordion. "But, Boomer," he went on, still breathless, "I didn't leave your side for six weeks. Do you remember that? In the night, if you cried out for your father, I was there, sleeping right beside you. Every day after school, I was waiting outside to take your hand and walk you home. Remember the trip to Fatty's Funland? Boy, your mother didn't want me to take you, but I took you anyway. Because I knew how you were feeling. Through that whole time I knew how you were feeling, how lost, how scared, how afraid you were even to mention your father. And I suffered for you, more than I suffered for myself. I would have taken your pain, every drop of it, and carried it myself if I could have." Grampa held his chin high. He was almost smiling.

"This is too hard, Grampa."

"No," Grampa said. "No, Boomer."

"If I could only run. No matter how bad I'm feeling, running always makes me feel better. Sometimes I try to imagine running away from this—this thing." Webb struck his chest. "Just running and running. In the springtime, when everything is green and airy. I picture myself running the hills at Marshbank, my knees high, my arms pumping. So free." He stopped and shook his head. "I don't know what to do."

Grampa held out both hands imploringly. "Please, please, don't let yourself go on like this. It kills me to hear you talk like this. That's for old people like me. You're a fifteen-year-old boy with your whole life ahead of you, not a rickety old man with one lung. You're carefree. You haven't even broken anyone's heart yet." He slapped his forehead. "Boomer, Boomer, Boomer, I had no business letting this happen. Don't torture yourself."

"Like I have a choice," Webb said.

"You do have a choice. Listen to me." Grampa pushed his hands against his chest, wheezing. "I'm the one at fault. Blame me, not yourself."

"Sometimes I try," Webb said. "I honestly do, but what I did is always there. It's trapped inside me." He shook his head. "It won't go away."

"Look at me." Grampa seized Webb by the shoulders and shook him. "No one else will ever know. It's like it never happened. You just have to get control of your mind. How do you think Alexander conquered the entire Persian Empire? Not because he was stronger, not because he had thousands more men. He told himself a dozen times a day that it was his destiny to rule the world, that he was fulfilling his destiny, that the outcome of his success was assured. Tell yourself this, a dozen times, a hundred times a day—*you* were riding in the car one afternoon and *I* was driving. It so happens I'm not paying attention, and I go off on the shoulder and hit the little—"

Webb put up his hand. "Don't. Just don't mention her at all. Don't say her name. Don't even tell me if she dies. Promise me, Grampa."

Grampa nodded. "Okay. If you promise to let me take the punishment."

It never would had happened if Grampa hadn't let him drive. Webb would still be the fastest runner at Spratling. And Taffy Putnam would probably be out ice-skating or tobogganing on Christmas Day instead of wasting away in some hospital bed. It wasn't like Webb had forced him to turn the car over. Any sensible adult would have said no. It was true, wasn't it? His mother would have said no. His father, for sure, would have said no.

"Boomer?" Grampa insisted.

If Grampa was right, that changed everything. Webb could just let go of it—the guilt, the fear, the bad dreams. He could be like he was before the accident, worrying about dumb stuff like algebra. Grampa sounded so certain, he must be right. Webb nodded. "Okay. Okay, Grampa."

Webb was ready to get out of the house when Beefy picked him up after dinner. It was snowing lightly when they got to Maxie's—a Victorian house trimmed with hundreds of Christmas lights. She came running out as soon as Beefy pulled up. Webb leaned over and opened the back door for her and slid his leg off the seat onto the floor to make room for her.

"Hi again," she said, bringing the scent of gingerbread into the car. "Here." She slid across the seat and handed him a cookie and handed another over the front seat to Beefy. "Fresh out of the oven."

"You baked these?" Beefy said, talking with half the gingerbread man hanging out of his mouth.

"Um-hmm," she said. "I love to cook."

"Will you marry me?" Beefy said as he pulled out of the driveway. "You're gorgeous, you're rich, and you can cook."

When Maxie hesitated, he said, "Oops, sorry, Webb—were you going to pop the big question tonight?"

Webb groaned. "Just drive, will you?"

"Where to?"

"Aren't you picking up Monica?"

Beefy shook his head. He reached back and took Webb's cookie. "She's visiting all two hundred of her relatives tonight. So"—he bit the cookie—"it's just the three of us."

"Well . . ." Webb looked across the seat at Maxie, wishing his cast wasn't stuck between them like a tree limb. "You want to see a movie?"

"Can't," Beefy said between mouthfuls. "Closed for Christmas."

"Oh. Well, then . . ." Webb rubbed his forehead, wishing he had planned the evening a little better.

"We could go tobogganing," Beefy said. "Or ice-skating."

"Beefy!" Maxie hit him on the shoulder.

"No, really," Webb said, leaning toward her. "If you want to do that, I don't mind. We could go back and get your ice skates, and I could just hang around the rink and watch. That would be fine. You and Beefy go."

"Great," Beefy said.

"No," Maxie said. "If you can't skate, I don't want to go either. Let's just drive around."

"In this slop?" Beefy pointed at the snow, which was falling heavily now.

"It's beautiful," Maxie said. "We can look at all the Christmas decorations." She smiled across the seat at Webb. "Okay?"

"Sure," he said. He took a deep breath and reached out to take Maxie's hand. "Just drive, Jeeves," he said, trying to make a joke. But all he could think about was that he was holding Maxie's hand. He looked over at her, and she gave his hand a little squeeze.

They drove around for two hours, with Beefy grumbling all the way. "Don't tell anyone I drove around all night looking at Christmas ornaments."

"But this is so pretty," Maxie said, pointing at a house surrounded by a forest of golden lights. "I love looking at the lights, don't you?"

Webb smiled at her and nodded, enjoying watching Maxie more than the lights. He was trying to figure out how he could slide close enough to put his arm around her, but he wouldn't be able to get his leg out of the way. He thought about just kissing Maxie's hand. Would it be too corny? He leaned toward her. "Maxie?"

"Hey." Beefy stopped the car. "Could we go back to your house for some more gingerbread?"

Maxie and Webb looked at each other. "Now?" Webb asked.

"Geez, you guys, this night is one big snore. Aren't you bored stiff?"

Webb looked across at Maxie in her fuzzy white coat with the lights from the big evergreens casting a yellow glow on her hair. Quickly he brought her hand up and kissed it. "Yeah," he said. "We're bored stiff."

As Beefy turned the car around he started singing, " 'Rudolph the red-nosed reindeer . . . ,' " and Webb and Maxie joined in all the way to Maxie's house.

chapter 11

GRAMPA WAS driving Webb to his first physical therapy session, in Bolton, the next town over. He had put on a tie, as if they were celebrating an important occasion. "I told your mother I was going to drive this car again. She didn't want me to, thought I'd be too scared. But it's like falling off a bike. You gotta get back on." He took out his unlit cigarette, tapped it on the dash, and put it back in his mouth. "Where would this country be if the great leaders gave in to fear?"

Webb shoved his fists into his jacket pockets. He didn't want Grampa to talk about the accident at all. Nevertheless, to his surprise, he was getting used to the image of his grandfather at the wheel that day. Grampa had told the story so many times in front of Webb, to

Webb's friends, to the mailman, the checkout clerk at the grocery store. It was becoming a reality, just as Grampa had promised. But Webb was not good at talking about the accident himself. He couldn't offhandedly remark to Grampa, "This is the first time you've driven since your accident." He couldn't even say "since *the* accident." Unlike Grampa, he never mentioned that day in even the most oblique way. There were enough reminders in his life without talking about it. Now, he touched his right leg. He had only gotten his cast off the day before, and it was strange to feel the pressure of his fingers beneath his sweatpants. It was strange to be sitting in the front after months of riding in the back, with his cast stretched out on the seat. His leg, when it emerged from the cast, was flaky and shriveled-looking, a leg that belonged to someone else, a polio victim or some wizened old man. He had dreamed of getting his cast off, the feeling of freedom he would have, but it wasn't like that at all. He still had to use his crutches. He pressed down tentatively with his right foot. His whole leg ached.

Grampa pulled up in front of the clinic and turned off the car. "I'll just come in with you this first time. Make sure you're set up with someone. Sign you in, look the place over."

"No!" Webb snapped. "I already told you." He opened the door. "I can handle this." He shut the door, but it didn't catch. After several trips to the body shop, the passenger door was still not right. He slammed it hard. "This stupid car," he muttered, hobbling away.

"I'll just drive around, pick up a pizza with that coupon book. Might as well drive around while I can. While I still have a license," Grampa called after him.

Webb didn't look back. If he could have, he would have dropped his crutches and broken into a run. If it happened, it happened. What difference would it make anyway? Grampa only drove to the grocery store and back. But Grampa kept reminding him that he might lose his license, go to jail, get sued. He didn't want Webb to forget his noble sacrifice. Webb moved up the ramp to the sliding doors with the wheelchair stickers on them.

He took the elevator up to the second floor and pushed open the door marked OAKWOOD PHYSICAL THERAPY. Inside, there was a waiting area and a huge expanse of gray carpeting filled with exercise machinery like the gym had where he went with Beefy a few times. There were some people working out—mostly older ones. One bent-over old lady walked on the treadmill very slowly as if she was sleepwalking. A gray-haired woman was lying on the floor with her legs propped up on a giant rubber ball, doing sit-ups.

"Hi there." A bright-faced girl with red glasses smiled at Webb. Her name tag said her name was Amy. "Would you like to sign in?" She pushed a clipboard across the pink counter. "A therapist will be right with you."

Webb moved up to the counter and picked up a pen.

"First time?" she asked.

"Yeah." He bit his lip, wondering how she knew. He wondered what else she knew about him. "Nice place," he said, trying to sound at ease.

"Oh, you'll learn to hate it," she said, laughing.

He smiled nervously and sat down, picking up a copy of *Sports Illustrated*. But before he had a chance to open it, his name was called. He looked up into the pale, unsmiling face of Dylis Clark. Her plastic tag said, DYLIS in bright orange letters. His mouth dropped open. "What's the big idea?"

She gave him the barest hint of a smile. "The big idea is for you to get up on your crutches and follow me. This way," she said, and disappeared around the corner without a backward glance.

Webb looked at the counter girl, wild-eyed. "She's not—she's not going to work on me," he squealed. "She's only in the tenth grade."

Amy smiled. "She's just an aide. She'll take you to your therapist." Still grinning, she pointed in the direction Dylis had gone.

He nodded, red-faced, and picked up his crutches. When he went into the gym he saw her standing outside a doorway on the edge of the room. He looked around to see if there was any other official-looking person who could help him, but there were only old people hobbling around the area.

She spotted him. "In there!" she called, pointing

with her pen at the door she was standing next to. "Go in and lie down. Ken will be with you shortly. And take off those pants," she added.

He looked at her.

"You did wear shorts, didn't you? Like they told you to?"

It was her know-it-all attitude that really bugged Webb, the same attitude she adopted in class when she got on her save-the-dolphins soapbox. "You probably don't know that dolphins are mammals. You probably think they're fish." She would start out smug and superior no matter what she was talking about. "Americans are the most wasteful people in the world. They throw away enough aluminum every three months to rebuild our entire commercial air fleet. *Most* Americans," she would add, leaving no doubt who the exception was. Dylis Clark harangued everyone for polluting the water, for being crassly materialistic, for not writing letters to their congressional representatives to save the dolphins. Not that anyone disagreed with her. She was just too intense. Webb almost felt sorry for her as she scurried down the hallways of school, passing out her latest flyers to anyone who didn't run the other way.

Now he gave her a big, fake smile. "Do they pay you to boss people around, or do you do that for free?" He crutched past her toward the doorway, but when he passed her his crutch struck the base of a gray, four-armed contraption beside her and he stumbled, just barely catching himself. He was so angry at Dylis and angry at his clumsiness in front of her that he entered the room and slammed the door behind him. He sank down on the white-sheeted table, letting both crutches clatter to the floor.

"Whoa—was it something I said?"

Webb jumped and looked behind him. There was a big, muscly guy with a full head of curly black hair, and one thick eyebrow across his forehead. "This is a regular haunted house."

The man laughed. "Some people think so. Some people call it a torture chamber." He stuck out his hand. "Ken Olivetti. And you are Webber Freegy."

Webb shook Ken's hand.

"So, Webb, you look like the impatient type. I'll bet you're anxious to get started."

Webb nodded. "I'm anxious to have a leg again instead of something that looks like a—a—"

"Piece of spaghetti?" Ken said. "You thought it would be strong as the hind leg of a bull, yeah? That you could hit the ski slopes this weekend. Maybe tackle the black diamonds?"

Webb smiled in spite of himself. "It would be nice to walk around without those." He nodded at the crutches.

Ken picked them up and leaned them against the wall. "You'll still need these for the next few weeks. Then you'll be free as a bird. That is, if you do your exercises at home and show up here three times a week. Understood?"

Webb nodded.

"So, okay." Ken clapped his hands together. "Today we're going to check you out. See how strong that leg is. Test your flexibility. You got a pair of shorts under this?"

Webb slid off his sweatpants, and Ken motioned him over to a scale at the end of the room. Webb hobbled over and stood on it, putting most of his weight on his good leg. He weighed 130, down five pounds from the accident.

"Okay, now stand on this with your left leg." Ken moved a block of wood up next to the scale. "And stand on the scale with your right leg. See how much weight you can take before it hurts."

Webb first put all his weight on his good leg, then gradually shifted weight to his right leg. It hurt almost immediately, but he shifted more weight until he could feel his right leg trembling.

"About eighty on the good leg, fifty on the bad," Ken said. "That leg still looks pretty shaky. We don't want to overdo it. It's going to take a while until you can support all one hundred thirty pounds on your right leg. You're not halfway there yet."

"How long?" Webb asked, his heart sinking. "I've got to run track in the spring for my school."

"A runner, huh?" Ken sat in a chair at the foot of the table. "That's good. I like the highly motivated ones. Let's see." He opened up a folder on the table beside him. "Mmmm. Fractured tibia and fibula, torn ligaments, fractured skull, concussion, contusions. Tsk, tsk." He looked back at Webb. "Auto accident?"

"Doesn't it say in there?" Webb gestured at the folder, anxious to know how much information there was on him.

"Nope." Ken shook his head. "Is it a secret?"

"No," Webb said quickly. "It was an auto accident." He took a deep breath. "I got hit by a car." He said it without thinking. It was a stupid lie, totally unnecessary, but he felt a little lightness in his chest when Ken looked at him sorrowfully.

"That's tough, Webb, really tough." Then Ken said, "You want to talk about it?"

The moment of warmth was replaced by a flutter of fear. "No," Webb said. "Not right now."

"So, okay," Ken said, clapping his hands again. "We're going to test your flexibility, see how much work that leg can do. And then we'll gradually build up your strength with exercise, weights. Remember, we're not going for pain here, Webb. We're going for no pain. This isn't track. It isn't running until your guts ache. We do everything slowly. It might take two months, it might take four or five months. Even longer."

"It won't take longer," Webb said.

"Good." While Webb was lying on the table, Ken held his leg out horizontally and gently bent his knee, pumping his leg up and down. "That hurt?" he asked.

"A little," Webb said, though it hurt more than a little. He wasn't going to go slow, he was going to go fast, get through therapy and get on with his life. He could do way more than most of those old people out there. He could stand a little pain. And the sooner he got better, the less he'd have to see of badger-face Dylis. God, he hoped she didn't work here on the same afternoons he came. Maybe she just worked Mondays. Ken had him turn over on his stomach and pumped his knee from behind. Webb groaned in spite of himself, and Ken eased off immediately.

"There's this girl who works here," Webb said, turning back over. "She goes to my school."

"That right?" Ken said. "Now sit on the edge of the table and bend your leg back as far as you can. Can you lift it up? Toward your nose, that's right. Slowly, slowly."

"Her name is Dylis," he said, lifting his leg and breaking into a sweat at the slice of pain.

"Dylis?" Ken said, making a note in his folder. "Dylis? Is that the—"

"Yeah," Webb said, "the fat one." He snorted.

Ken didn't laugh. "Is she on tonight? I'll have her show you the machines just so you'll be more familiar with them when we get started on Wednesday."

"Oh, no," Webb said quickly, trying to sit up. He winced and lay back down. "I just wondered what her work schedule is. No big deal."

Ken had his own agenda. "I want you to do these exercises at home," he said. "We'll go over them and then let you have a look at the gym." He handed Webb some pages with pictures of skinny men in shorts, pushing against a wall or curled into a ball on the floor. In one picture the guy looked like a pointer dog, kneeling on one leg with the other leg bent up behind him. Ken had Webb try the exercises one at a time.

"We do this for running," Webb said, "but not against a wall."

"That's right," Ken said. "The wall will help give that leg support. You might not be able to do it at first."

He was right. Webb's right leg wouldn't hold him, even leaning against a wall. "God, I'm such a feeb," Webb said, panting with the effort.

"Don't get discouraged," Ken said. "You'll see progress every week. Don't judge yourself by what you used to do. Just remember, you're learning to walk all over again. Just go easy. Now, let's get that aide."

"Never mind," Webb said, but Ken disappeared out the door.

He came back with Dylis. "Just briefly show him the machines, okay? I'll set him up on Wednesday. You can handle that, can't you?" He looked at Dylis.

"Most assuredly," she said earnestly.

Webb groaned inwardly. The only person who ever said "most assuredly" was his doddering old biology teacher. "If you turn the flame all the way up, students, you will most assuredly defeat the purpose of this experiment."

"Right this way," Dylis said to Webb. She led him over to where a fat man was pedaling on an exercise bike, rocking slowly from side to side like he was riding through heavy mud. "The exercise bike," she announced. "But you're not ready for this yet. I can tell by the way you're leaning into those crutches."

"Listen," Webb said, trying to sound casual, "I appreciate the tour and everything, but I have to get going. My ride will be here."

"Suit yourself." She walked away.

Webb looked at his watch. Grampa wouldn't be along for another twenty minutes. He crutched over to the waiting area and pulled on his sweatpants, which he had draped around his neck. The girl behind the desk was gone. Webb slumped down in a chair and jiggled his left leg up and down. Then he jiggled his right leg to test the difference. He didn't think he was leaning *that* heavily on his crutches. He leaned forward and wiggled his kneecap back and forth. More pain. He sighed. With both hands he lifted his leg from the floor and held it out for ten seconds.

"I see you're still here."

Webber dropped his leg as if Dylis had caught him doing something illegal.

She shoved her hair back roughly with both hands. "Taffy Putnam—"

Webb lifted his eyes and stared at her, not breathing.

"I'm her baby-sitter. Once a week for three years. Ever since she was seven." Dylis licked her lips, then blotted them with the back of her hand, not taking her eyes from Webb's.

Webb felt the crushing weight in his chest.

"I'll bet you didn't know that, did you?"

He took a gulp of air, conscious of a hammering inside his head, like a wild, repeating message in Morse code. It rose to a crescendo, drowning out the piped-in music in the background. Finally he shook his head. "No."

"Well . . . ," she said, and he could tell she was going to keep talking. He wanted to stop her, to get away from her. He reached for his crutches, but he wasn't fast enough.

"I used to baby-sit her every Sunday afternoon. We had this routine where we'd go to the park behind her house if it was a nice day. I was the queen and she was my servant, and I'd sit on the merry-go-round, and she would have to push me around and around until I told her to stop. She was so fast, fast as a whip, and she never got tired, never asked if she could quit running." Dylis was talking fast, saying the words like she was reciting an advertising jingle, something that had no meaning to her. But even though her face was rigid, her cheeks and then her whole face broke out in red splotches as she went on. "I'd just sit there being this fat queen and watch her race around and around, her braids flying out from her face. My dad and I went to visit her last week," she said abruptly.

Webb wanted to put his fingers in his ears, wanted to shout at the top of his lungs to keep from hearing what she was going to say. "I gotta go," he said, lunging for his crutches.

But Dylis went on, faster than before, her eyes boring into Webb's face. "She was lying there in this big bed with tubes all over her, not moving, not making a sound. I tried to talk to her, to just get her to nod her head if she heard me but she couldn't even do that. Her face was all—" Dylis pulled her lips into a tight 0, stretching the skin on her face so that it was smooth and shiny. "She didn't look like a little girl at all. She looked like a rubber ball that somebody drew a face on. I asked her if she wanted to go back to the park with me, and you know what she did?" Dylis had been staring at Webb, talking without emotion like she had been wound up. When she stopped, her eyes filled with tears. She swiped at them angrily. When she spoke again, her voice was trembling. "She whimpered. Like a little—a little lost rabbit."

She looked at Webb, and her face crumpled like he had punched her hard in the stomach. "I just wanted to tell you," she said without a trace of sarcasm in her voice. Then she turned and walked away, leaving Webb all alone in the empty room.

chapter 12

WHEN HIS father died so suddenly, Webb had told Grampa he wanted to go to Fatty's Funland in Tennessee. He'd seen it on TV. And Grampa had told his mother, "He will never, for the rest of his life, have his father to hang around with, to take him places. From now on, it's only me. I was a lousy father to my own son—either at the grocery all day or out at the track. No time to read him a story, play ball with him, watch him grow up—his mother raised him single-handed. But I'm not going to make that mistake with Boomer. I'm gonna be a helluva father to my grandson. He needs me, Ches. He needs me to take him out of this misery for a few days." Those days went by so fast, Webb thought of his father only at night when Grampa sat staring out at the moon. That was the only bad time. As long as they were running around, keeping busy, Webb was fine. And as long as they didn't talk about it.

Webb didn't tell anyone about his conversation with Dylis. Besides, he and Grampa had their agreement. Taffy Putnam was unmentionable, just like certain parts of his father's death were unmentionable. The worst parts, no one in the family talked about. Not even Grampa, who bragged to everyone from the Avon lady to the pharmacist, that his son had died saving another man from drowning. Webb felt a steely hand grip his heart whenever he thought of his father under the ice, struggling for air. He would move his mind somewhere else, shake his fingers, sing a wordless little tune.

That gripping pain had come back when Dylis told him about Taffy Putnam. He had to rush out into the snowy night and crutch up and down the sidewalk until Grampa arrived.

That night he hung around the kitchen, eating pizza and talking with his mother and Grampa. "It's not that Beefy's a bad worker, he just can't do anything on an empty stomach," his mother said. "This afternoon he got powdered sugar all over Mrs. Voorheis's drapes."

"I'll be back in a couple of weeks," Webb promised. "As soon as I'm off these crutches."

"Well, it'll be a relief," she told him, laughing. "Keeping Beefy in doughnuts is going to bankrupt me."

"Sarasota," the radio announcer said, "has just been

trounced by Hurricane Kristin, and she's moving south at a hundred miles an hour."

"Saragossa," Grampa announced, as if that was what the weatherman had said, "that was a city in Spain. Did I ever tell you the story of Charlemagne's great defeat on his way back from the City of Gold? That's what Saragossa was—the City of Gold."

Webb and his mother exchanged long-suffering looks. "No," Webb said, taking another piece of pizza. "We haven't heard that one." But instead of being bored, he was comforted by the familiar story, by the lifting and falling of Grampa's voice. It was like a lullaby to Webb. It felt good to be inside, away from the storm, which was picking up speed as the night wore on. Outside, the wind blew sleet against the window with a steady, cracking sound. He imagined, with a shiver, being out in the weather, alone, with no place to go, and he turned his chair away from the window, concentrating instead on the hot, cheesy taste of the pizza. He ate it slowly, listening to Grampa's voice, savoring everything around him. His eyes traveled across the white, glass-fronted cupboard full of his mother's castle dishes, her pink-and-white cups and plates. He had been eating off those same plates since he was little, sitting in the kitchen on winter nights listening to Grampa's same stories. He loved the way everything in the kitchen had stayed the same—the red teakettle, the big white bowl painted with cherries that his father had bought for his mother in Detroit. The shaky, frightened feeling that he

140

had felt earlier dropped away. He felt safe again. He could stay there forever, he thought, listening to Grampa's voice.

Then his mother turned to him, her gold hair shining under the lights. "I can't believe I forgot to ask how your therapy went," she said, rapping herself on the head with the palm of her hand.

Webb was catapulted back to the waiting room with Dylis. He put down his pizza.

"Nothing to it," he said. "The same kind of exercises I do in track. This guy Ken, my therapist, says I'll be back in shape for track, no problem. I just have to do my exercises."

His mother patted his cheek. "Attaboy."

Grampa punched his arm. "Hey, this guy Ken doesn't know what a trouper he's got."

Webb turned and looked back outside. They thought he was wonderful. No matter what happened they always thought he was wonderful.

The next day he returned to his old routines at school. Without the cast to drag around, he could sit in the back of his classes again. He felt more comfortable—making jokes with his pals, watching the girls up front combing their hair and passing notes back and forth. Sometimes, during a lull, he remembered what Dylis had said, and it took his breath away. Why did she have to tell him about Taffy Putnam, how broken up she was? Did she want Webb to suffer more? Did she think he needed to be punished? No, he thought,

141

drawing his mind away. Think of something else. And he would start whistling under his breath the way he used to when he thought about his father drowning.

After English he met Maxie at his locker and walked her to the cafeteria. This was their routine now. He called her almost every night after his exercise, and at school she waited for him between classes. He liked seeing Maxie standing next to his locker as he came down the hall, liked that she was waiting for him, that she laughed so easily at his jokes.

"Hi, Webbie," she said, giving him a big smile. "Tell your grampa that was a great dinner. And I can't believe you made that onion soup."

"Maxie," he said, leaning his crutches against the locker, "all the world's great chefs are men. Admit it."

She crossed her arms over her chest and gave him a look.

"Ooops," he said, grinning. "I take it back. Even James Beard couldn't measure up to Pasta Gallagher." When he'd been invited to Maxie's for dinner, Mrs. Gallagher had made dessert, but Maxie had done everything else, including a great shrimp pasta. He took off his book bag and dropped it, then opened his locker door. A globe bounced out on the gray tile. It was a beach ball globe, blue and green for oceans and land, with circles and arrows all over it in purple marker.

Maxie picked it up. "What are all these purple marks for?"

Webb hadn't really looked at the globe for a couple

of years. When he was in the seventh grade, Grampa had marked the military routes of Alexander the Great on the globe for a talk Webb was giving in his history class. Grampa had practically written his entire speech. He was more excited than Webb when Webb got the highest mark in the class. Now Webb took the globe from Maxie. "Those are the places I plan to live."

"Visit?" she said.

"No, live." He stuffed the globe back in his locker and rummaged around till he found his lunch. As soon as he said it, Webb knew it was true. He couldn't stay in Lemon Lake forever. He would move away as soon as he graduated. "I think I'd like to live in Spain for a while," he said. "Saragossa, Spain, the City of Gold." He pictured himself there, riding a horse through a mountain pass, with saddlebags full of gold. Nobody would know him there. He might even go by another name. Charley or Alex.

"Gol, Webber," Maxie said, rooting around in the bottom of his locker. "This is a mess. I'll bet you don't know half the stuff that's in here." She pulled out a string of dried chili peppers and held it up.

"Hey, aloha." He draped it around her neck and kissed her on the cheek.

Pulling it off, she dropped it over Webb's head.

"I forgot I had this," he said. "Next time you come over, Grampa and I will make you blowtorch chili. That'll knock your socks off." He shut his locker, and they headed for the lunchroom.

"What's wrong with living in Lemon Lake?" she asked.

"It's too small," he said, because he couldn't think of anything else to say.

"I like Lemon Lake," Maxie said. "I can just imagine sending my kids to the drugstore for some ice cream, and there is Mr. Pushkin, standing behind the counter in his white apron, same as ever. And he says, 'Well, little missy. What can I do for you?'" She laughed. "I mean, it drives you crazy, but it makes you feel you belong here."

Webb groaned. "It drives you crazy. Period." But he was somewhere else, riding a horse through a mountain pass, camping under a waterfall in South America.

Maxie set his lunch bag down on the table across from Beefy, gave him a wave, and disappeared into the food line.

"Your slave," Beefy said, watching her go.

"You're just jealous," Webb said.

Beefy pointed at the chili peppers. "Is it your weirdness she's attracted to?"

Webb touched the peppers. "One of many reasons," he said. He unwrapped his dill pickle and slid it inside his bologna sandwich. Suddenly he was looking into Dylis Clark's face. Webb felt the steely fist take hold of his heart. He put down his sandwich. He knew Dylis had to walk by his table to get to her usual spot in the back of the room.

Webb turned to Beefy with sudden enthusiasm. "Did

you ever eat a whole chili pepper?" He ripped one off and held it up in front of his lips.

"Hey, I'll give you a buck if you eat that," Beefy said, grinning.

Webb bit the chili and felt nothing. He took another bite and started chewing. "Nothing to it." Suddenly there was so much heat in his mouth he felt like he had swallowed a burning match. "Aaauuuh," he said, gasping for air. Quickly, before he could change his mind, he shoved the rest of the chili in his mouth and chewed, his mouth a cavern of fire. When Dylis passed his table he grinned at her, ripped off another chili pepper, and put it in his mouth whole. Tears were pouring down his cheeks.

Dylis looked at him, then looked away with a sour expression.

"God, Webber, you should see your face. You look like a dragon." Beefy was laughing so hard other kids turned to look. "Look at Freegy, he's eating those peppers whole. He's going to croak. He's going to erupt."

After Dylis passed, he drank his pop in one long chug. Then he picked up Beefy's and finished it. He opened his mouth wide and drew in a long, shuddering breath, but the furnace was still in his mouth, his throat, all the way down to his stomach. Kids were standing around him in a circle, ripping off more peppers for him to eat. "Here, dragon mouth."

Webb didn't feel like eating another pepper just then, but he was glad Dylis was watching him from over in the corner. She didn't know the first thing about having fun, acting goofy. If his mouth burned for two days, at least he had shown Dylis Clark that she wasn't going to ruin his life.

On Wednesday at therapy, after Ken set him on the treadmill, Webb pushed the pace up a few notches. He wasn't one of those old codgers who could barely walk, he thought. But he gripped the railing with both hands to take pressure off his bad leg. It ached with every step. He kept his eyes ahead of him, hoping that if Dylis was working he wouldn't see her. She came by with a stack of towels and stopped next to him. She held out a towel.

Webb let go of the railing and winced as he took it and draped it around his neck.

"Your leg looks pretty weak," she said.

He ignored her.

She stood there for a minute, not saying a word. Finally she said, "You should slow down."

His first instinct was to reach out and turn up the speed, but he stopped himself. Pretend she isn't there, he told himself. He imagined he was walking around the shore of Lemon Lake, cooling down after a ten-mile run. The sun was out, drying the sweat on his face. He felt good, strong and fast. He pictured the feel of the grass brushing his legs, the sound of birds chattering in the trees overhead. He would stop when he got to the docks and stretch out on the gray planks to do push-ups. His leg was stronger than ever. "Hey!" he yelled. Dylis had reached over and turned down the speed. He let go of the railing to reset the dial, stumbled, and went down. The treadmill shot him backward, off the end, and onto the floor.

"What did you do that for?" he snarled, trying to stand up.

Just then Ken came up. "You okay?" He helped Webb stand. "Take a little break, Webber. You were going pretty fast."

Webb leaned over his crutches, trying to get his breath. "I was fine until she screwed it up." He still didn't look at Dylis.

"You were going too fast," she said behind him.

"C'mon over here and sit in the Biodex," Ken said. "Take some pressure off that knee." He followed Webb over to the machine.

"She acts like she owns the place," he muttered to Ken. "She ought to shut up and hand out towels like she's paid to do."

"She means well," Ken said. He started fiddling with the adjustments on the machine, and Webb could see that Dylis wasn't going to get the chewing-out she deserved. A man in baggy purple shorts came by and watched him for a few minutes. Webb didn't look at him, and pretty soon the guy limped away. He finished his session in silence, not looking at anyone. The skinny guy in the purple shorts had gone over to the lady working with the beach ball. They were laughing like they were having an evening at the circus. Webb couldn't wait to get out of there, away from all the old fogeys.

At five o'clock, as he was leaning against a wall pulling his sweats back on, Dylis showed up again. He glared at her. "Go knock somebody else down, Clark."

"Ken wants me to apologize," she said reluctantly.

Webb snorted. "Don't do me any favors."

"I was trying to help you, Webber. You were going too fast."

"I'm touched by your concern." Webb took his crutches and shoved them under his arms.

"Well, I'm sorry you fell down," she said uneasily.

"Sorry you made me fall down." He crutched past her. For the first time in his life, he'd had the last word with Dylis Clark.

chapter 13

WEBB WORKED doggedly on his exercises at home. Across his mirror he taped up all the pictures Ken had given him of the skinny guy doing exercises. Underneath, he taped all the printouts from Ken—knee flexions, extensions, leg raises, extensions, abductions— exercises that Webb did nightly, in sets of ten. He worked for an hour a night, until he lay panting on the floor in a puddle of sweat, his radio blaring from the dresser. Sometimes, when he didn't think he could pick himself up off the floor to take a shower, he would talk himself into another set. "Ten more extensions, Webber. You can do it, you can do it." It was how he talked to himself when he was running. "Come up, Webber. Pick up the pace a notch. You can do it." And he would drag himself up on his knees and start counting. But going to the clinic took away his heart.

It was Dylis Clark. He would go to the clinic all pumped up, knowing he had to put everything into his exercises, knowing that by Wednesday at the latest, he would be able to pitch his crutches forever, because his leg was feeling stronger than ever and he could make it from one end of the house to the other with only a slight limp. But when he got to the clinic, he would stand on the scale with his left leg and, ever so slowly, shift his weight until his right leg was shaking like a plucked string.

"You're nearly at sixty-five pounds," Ken would say. "Another couple weeks and you can get rid of these things."

Dylis was like a disease the way she drained his energy. She reminded him of a cartoon in his health book of the swine-flu bacteria—a pig with a menacing grin and a pitchfork, waiting to attack someone. It was okay that she didn't like him. But she wanted him to fail, he could sense it. She would be perfectly happy if he had to limp around on crutches for the rest of his life. He started bringing his own towel from home so he wouldn't need anything from her. But Dylis would sneak up on him while he was doing squats or working at the unweighting machine. He could feel her little pig eyes staring at him, feel her wanting him to fall over, wanting his leg to go out from under him.

"Shaky," she'd say grimly. "Very shaky. You'll never

make any progress unless you take off some of that weight."

Webb never spoke to Dylis. He avoided looking at her. But he listened as she made her way around the room, passing out towels, talking to other patients. She was different with them. "Hey, Mr. Van Goebel," she called out to a fat guy who had fractured his elbow. He could barely bend his arm. "See if you can catch this." She threw a beach ball across the room and clapped her hands when he caught it. "Barry Sanders," she said, hooting like she was a stand-up comic.

Webb groaned, but Mr. Van Goebel broke up. He liked her, Webb thought in amazement. There were people in this room who actually liked Dylis Clark. When he did try to make a few friends at the center, Dylis managed to ruin that too.

Al, the guy with the purple shorts, was working on the unweighting machine next to the treadmill, where Webb was. "When I first came here," he said to Webb, "I couldn't lift this arm any higher than my waist. Couldn't lift a beer can to my lips." Al was one of the most active people there, moving from machine to machine like a kid at a carnival, chatting with everyone as he puffed his way through the exercises. "I can go shoulder-high now," he continued. "Look."

Webb glanced over, nodded, as Al let go of the lever he was pulling on and it went clattering behind him. Al held out his right arm level with his shoulders to demonstrate.

"What'd you do?" Webb asked, more out of politeness than curiosity.

"Oh, man, it was rough." Al shook his head and reached back for the levers. "I was thrown by a bucking horse. Landed on my shoulder. Whoof," he said, with the exertion of pulling the lever forward. "Whoof." He grabbed the other lever.

Webb looked at him again. He was bald and skinny, wrinkled as a prune. He had to be almost as old as Grampa. "Wow!" he exclaimed admiringly. "I can't believe it."

"Good!" Al hooted. "Because I haven't been on a horse in sixty years. I fell out of bed. Drunk." He threw back his bald head and laughed.

Something bubbled up in Webb, a lightness he hadn't felt in months. He grinned back at Al and started to laugh too. Annie, the red-haired lady who always worked out with the beach ball, sat up on the floor next to them and laughed too, the ball bouncing up and down on her belly. "Don't you be corrupting this young, innocent boy with your lies," she said, pointing a finger at Al. "He brought it on himself," she said to Webber. "I have no sympathy."

"You got no sympathy for no one," Al said, dropping his arms and sitting forward on the bench. "You're a stony-hearted woman."

"Ah," Annie said, looking at Webb, "you're wrong. I have sympathy for this adorable young man with the muscles." She squeezed the beach ball suggestively.

"This one was struck by a car, a drunk driver almost eclipsed his young life, almost sent him up into the arms of St. Peter."

"Holy moly." Al whistled between his teeth and leaned over to pat Webb on the back as he trotted along the treadmill. "I might be an old drunk, but I never ran over no one. Was this an old drunk like me," he asked Webb, "or a young one?"

Webb hesitated. He had told Annie the story the previous Wednesday when Ken was working with him on the leg-flexing machine. "Hey, Ken," she had said, flopping down beside them with her beach ball, "who's your handsome friend?"

"Annie, meet Webber," Ken said. He looked at Webb. "Get on her good side. She makes the best toffee crunch you ever ate."

Webb was polite and answered a barrage of questions about his age, where he went to school, whether he played tennis. And then she asked, right in front of Ken, "How did you hurt your leg, honey?"

"Auto accident," Webb mumbled.

"Somebody hit you, is that it?" She had red glasses the color of her hair, and she came over and peered in his face, her eyes magnified behind her lenses.

Webb glanced at Ken. "Yeah."

"Well, sweetie, was there alcohol involved? Was the driver who hit you drinking?"

It was easier to just nod. Saying no would have required an explanation. And, he had to admit, he liked the warm rush of sympathy when Annie took him by the hand, her face crumpled in sorrow. "You poor thing. You poor little thing—you're lucky to be alive."

Now Webb was forced to embellish the story even further to answer Al's question. "An old one," he said quietly. "He was an older man."

"My age?" Al persisted. "Was this drunken fool who ran you down and busted your leg as old as I am?"

Webb lifted his eyes from the treadmill to look at Al, and there was Dylis staring at him in the mirror. Dylis opened her mouth like she was going to say something, then closed it in a hard line. She handed a towel to Al, one to Annie. Then she said it. "I didn't know your grandfather was drinking when he hit Taffy. I thought you said he wasn't drinking."

Webb's heart started racing so fast he felt light-headed. He was caught. He had told the lie in front of everyone, and Dylis had caught him. He tried to think of something to say, conscious of Al looking at him with a half-grin on his face, Annie getting to her knees and bouncing her beach ball—waiting for him to explain why he'd said he was hit by a drunk driver when he hadn't been hit at all. When his grandfather hadn't been drinking at all. When his grandfather hadn't been driving at all.

"He—" Webb clutched the rails of the treadmill, his feet striking the surface like a hammer driving a nail into his heart. *Bam, bam, bam, bam.* He turned off the machine. "I gotta use the john." And, leaving his crutches propped against the leg flexer, he limped away from all of them.

He went to the men's room and stood there with his hands on the sink, breathing hard. You didn't just say something like that to purposely humiliate someone. You made allowances for people. How many times had he let Grampa's exaggerations slide by, listened to tall tales get taller? Once, Grampa told someone that *he,* Grampa, had gone out on the ice and pulled a man out of the freezing water. And Webb had let it go. Sometimes the words that came out of his own mouth surprised him. He hadn't meant that he had been hit by a drunk driver. The woman had interpreted it that way. She'd trapped him.

Webb hung his head and clutched the sides of the sink. "God," he said, "when is this going to end?" Taking a deep breath, he lifted his head, looking at himself in the mirror. His brown hair was plastered with sweat against his forehead. His pale face made his eyes stand out like blue marbles. His nose, if you lined it up with a hundred other noses, was unremarkable—not huge and red like Grampa's, but narrow and squarish, with a little flare at the nostrils. It reminded him of the wooden clothespins his mother used in her shop. There were a few pimples on his face, but nothing to get excited about. There was *nothing* there to get excited about, he thought. He didn't wear a nose ring. No tattoos. He was ordinary as grass. Why was this happening to him?

As he stood there at the sink he had a flash of a memory: his first day of school, and Grampa and his father were walking him down the sidewalk, one on either side, each holding a hand, and they were telling him about kindergarten.

"You tell them your name is Freegy," Grampa was saying. "Be proud of that."

"Tell them you can print your name and sing 'The Star-Spangled Banner,' " his father said.

"And run around the block five times without stopping," said Grampa.

"And moo," said his father.

As they went on, Webb's heart grew heavier and heavier. He thought of how disappointed all the boys and girls in his new classroom would be after they found out how ordinary he really was. Even though he fooled his father and grandfather, he knew he couldn't fool all those kids he didn't know. He yanked his hands back and broke away from Grampa and his father. He turned around and started running back home, back to his mother, who knew he was just an ordinary five-year-old boy who still wet the bed almost every night.

"Hey, Webber." Ken walked into the bathroom now, put his hand on Webb's shoulder. "You doggin' it in here?"

Webb shook his head.

"C'mon, buddy," Ken slipped his arm around Webb's neck in a vise grip. "Mrs. Wallaker sent me in here for you. Watching your lithe young body doing squats gives her the trembles. You've got your public to consider."

Webb followed Ken out of the bathroom and stopped at the purple padded board to do standing leg curls for the rest of the hour. He kept his eyes lowered and didn't speak to anyone.

At the end of the session Webb collapsed in a chair by the waiting area to towel off his face before he went out in the cold. He sat there for a moment with his face in the towel. How could he get out of therapy? Better he should be helping his mother at her drapery shop for those seven or eight hours a week. It was time for him to get back into life.

"Well, hello, Webber."

He lifted his face from the towel and looked up at a policeman. It was the cop who had visited Webb at the hospital. Webb sucked in his breath. Had the cop traced him here? "H-Hi." Webb sat up straighter.

"Officer Mike Clark." He shook Webb's hand and sat down beside him. "Dylis said you were coming here."

Webb blinked. "She called you? She told you I was here?" His voice broke on the last word.

Officer Clark smiled. "Dylis is my daughter." He pulled back his blue sleeve and looked at his watch. "I'm a little early, for a change."

Webb nodded, still breathless with fear that Officer

Clark had really come for him, that he was trying to throw Webb off with the story about Dylis. "Well—" Webb stood up.

"Can I give you a lift? We live near you—the corner of Pacific and Jones."

"My grandfather is waiting."

Officer Clark studied him for a moment. "You doing okay, Webber? Getting around on that leg now?"

Webb nodded and walked out, limping down the hall to the elevator before he remembered his crutches. He kept going. Until he was downstairs in the lobby, he was certain that Officer Clark was going to come after him. He could almost feel the weight of that big hand falling on his shoulder. *"Oh, Webber, one more thing . . ."* Webb pushed through the doors, spotted Grampa, and scrambled into the front seat of the car.

"Boomer," Grampa said, reaching over him to slam the door, "I saw that cop again. He was just here." Grampa pointed at the building to indicate where Clark had gone. As they took off, he turned the wheel sharply and Webb fell against his shoulder. "I wonder what he's nosing around for?" Grampa reached down and turned on the headlights as they pulled out onto the road.

Webb felt how the night pressed down on the two of them, even through the windshield of the car. He shuddered, fearing that it would crush the glass and smother them both. Closing his eyes, he tried to take a deep breath, but he couldn't. He lifted his eyes to the naked branches rattling in the February wind and the star-scattered sky beyond. Then he realized it wasn't the night oppressing him. It was something else. Dylis had heard him say that his grandfather had been drinking that afternoon. That he had been drunk. And Dylis's father was Officer Clark.

chapter 14

WEBBER WAS riding through Saragossa, the City of Gold; riding a white horse whose black saddlebags were filled with gold; wearing a gold crown studded with gems that glittered in the sunlight. People, mobs of them, lined the street, tossing gold coins and shouting his name. At the end of the street he could see the Hollywood Market on one corner and Porky's Diner at the other. Between the rooftops stretched a huge red banner that said, FINISH LINE. Galloping, galloping toward the finish line, people cheering, saddlebags jingling— Webber coaxed his steed onward. "Faster, faster, faster," he urged, clutching at the white mane. He was almost there, almost the winner, when a little girl, with braids flying, stumbled into the cobbled street. Webber couldn't rein in the horse. Its hooves came crushing down on her.

Webb woke, sweaty and exhausted, his fists clenched like he was in a boxing match. Outside, it was dark, but he hoped it was near dawn, because he knew he wouldn't get back to sleep. He never did after the dreams. He didn't even try anymore. Sitting up in bed, he looked out the window. He sat there feeling feverish and sick, seeing only the replay of his dream. After a long time, the lights from the marina appeared in his vision far out beyond the big dock.

It was the end of February and the ice was still frozen, buried under a foot and a half of snow. Tracks from skis and snowmobiles crisscrossed the lake as far as the eye could see. In a few weeks this giant surface would all turn to mush, he thought. It would all slide back down into the lake, like ice cubes in a glass of water. Then nobody would be on it. Nobody with a grain of sense. In March, Webb thought. March was when the man had gone out fishing. His name was Jack Asbury. Everyone on the lake knew when the ice was safe and when it was too early in the season or too late. Everyone but Jack Asbury. "Jackass Bury," his mother called him.

He looked at the clock radio on his nightstand. Five A.M. He plugged his earphones in and turned on the radio to drown out the dream, to drown out Jack Asbury and everything else.

After school Webb went to Chessie's Needles, his mother's shop. He went there now on Tuesdays and

Thursdays and all day on Saturdays. Today she was measuring someone for a bridesmaid's dress. "Oh, this color will look lovely on you, with your eyes and your olive complexion," she was saying to the young woman as she snugged a measuring tape across her ample bosom. His mother was good with people, Webb thought as he refolded a bolt of plaid fabric and carried it to the other end of the room to the stacks. She said the same kinds of things to everyone—that they had wonderful taste, that the drapes they chose were the prettiest, the most elegant. But it didn't seem insincere when she said it. She believed that she made people more beautiful, their homes more inviting.

Webb picked up an armload of green brocade, carried it over to the pressing table, and gave it to Millie, one of the seamstresses. He picked up another section of green drapery, half-listening to his mother as he carried it across the wooden floor.

". . . lovely figure," she was saying. "Perfect time of year for a wedding." Though he busied himself with the activity in the shop, Webb kept thinking of Dylis, what he would say to her. He had to convince her that what he'd said about Grampa wasn't true, that he hadn't been drinking before the accident. How could he have said such a jerky thing? he wondered, flinging the drape up over the line next to the pressing table. Now he had to suck up to jerky Dylis so she wouldn't tell her father that Grampa had been drinking. What could he say to her? "Dylis, I have always admired your lovely figure and olive complexion. I feel so fortunate that I get to see your smiling face here three days a week. And since we're such great friends, would you do me a weensy favor?" He snorted. With Dylis, that approach was doomed. He reached for the drape and knocked over a box of drapery pins, sending them flying all over the floor. He got down on one knee, wincing as he bent his right leg, and began picking them up. Maybe he should read up on dolphins, he thought. Offer a contribution to Save the Dolphins if she would set her father straight.

He stuck his finger on the end of a pin. "Dammit." The easiest thing would be to let it go. Say nothing and hope Dylis would forget what he had said. Or maybe her father wouldn't believe her anyway. He had gathered his own evidence, and he seemed to believe what Grampa had said. Webb remembered that Officer Clark had said Grampa had been very cooperative. But the hearing was three weeks from Friday. He couldn't take the chance that the lawyers would think his grandfather had been drunk. It was bad enough, Webb thought, that Grampa might go to jail for hitting Taffy Putnam.

A dull heaviness pressed down on him. Why had he told those lies to Al and Annie in the first place? And to Ken, about getting hit by a car? At the time it didn't seem to matter. But maybe it did, he thought. Maybe the truth did matter. Otherwise, how did you know, yourself, what was real? It was like convincing everyone that Grampa had been driving that day. Everyone else believed it. So it became real, didn't it? His mother believed it. Even Grampa believed it now. But if Webb hadn't been driving, he wouldn't have been telling all these lies. He shook his head to clear his thoughts. For a moment he stopped picking up the pins and ran his fingers over his face as if searching for the real Webber Freegy. He knew he wasn't who he used to be, and he knew he didn't like who he had become.

He didn't even like to be around Grampa anymore. Everything had changed between them. They didn't hang around in the kitchen together frying chicken, cooking up big pots of chili. How long had it been since he sat on the red stool, chopping onions, listening to Grampa shouting over his shoulder about saving St. Mary's from burning down? Now all he talked about was the hearing, about whether he would be sued, about going to jail.

Webb dropped the last pin into the box and pushed himself up off the floor, easing his knee back into position and stepping on the end of the slippery brocade as he did so. He went down again, grabbing at the fabric as his legs went out from under him. The sound of tearing fabric made every other sound in the shop stop.

"Webber!" his mother called, rushing forward. Millie set the iron down and came from behind the pressing board as Webb got to his feet. His mother, open-mouthed, stopped in her tracks when she saw the jagged tear in the ten-foot drapery. "Those drapes are supposed to be delivered this evening."

Webb stood dumbly, holding up the box of pins like

a torch. Beside him he heard Millie clicking her tongue. And the bridesmaid pointed, as if he couldn't see for himself. "He tore it," she said, "ruined that perfectly gorgeous drape."

Webb looked at his mother's horrified expression. "Can you fix it?" he asked hopefully.

She came forward and took the box of pins from his hand. Then she bent over to examine the drape on the floor. "Dammit, Webber," she said, and turned and marched back to the front of the store with the bridesmaid behind her.

"I'm sorry," Webb called after her. "I'll make it up somehow. I'll come in and work all day on Sunday." He slumped down on the work stool, massaging his knee. "Oaf," he mumbled. Saturday he had yanked a bolt of fabric out of the bottom of the stack and the momentum of the swinging bolt had knocked over the old dressmaker dummy and broke off her chin. He had come back to work to help his mother, but all he did was destroy things. Destroy everything in his path. He rubbed at his knee, wishing he could break through the front door and race down Rosetta Street, bareheaded and jacketless in the snow-sparkled afternoon. How he missed that feeling of freedom, that flying-forward-into-the-universe feeling that came from having legs that could cover five miles in an eye blink. Would he ever have it again? Would he ever walk like a normal human being again?

"Webbie!"

He looked up to see Maxie sweeping through the front door in a red cape and the red mittens he had bought her for Valentine's Day. She stopped to hug his mother, admire the bridesmaid's fabric. Webb smiled as she came down the aisle, but his heart dropped. He wasn't up to Maxie's cheeriness this afternoon. He wished he could slink out the back door.

"Hi, Maxie." He absorbed her hug, feeling the coldness of the outdoors surround him. "You look like Little Red Riding-Hood."

She stepped back and twirled, the cape billowing out around her. "You like it? Anyway, I was just down the street having my fingernail repaired, and I knew you were working this afternoon so"—she held out her arms—"Little Red Riding-Hood came to visit."

"Great," he said halfheartedly. "What did you do to your finger?"

"My finger*nail*. I broke it fitting the key in the ignition. I was practicing for driver training—oh, Webb, I can't believe you're waiting until summer to take it; now we won't have it together. Anyway," she went on breathlessly, "I had to come back and have a new one glued on and then repainted and"—she rolled her eyes—"what an ordeal for one little fingernail."

"Yeah," he agreed, thinking it was the understatement of the century.

"And I wondered if when you're off—like around nine—my dad and I could pick you up and we could buzz over to the club. He has to drop off some papers, and we could go in and I could show you around. We could grab something to eat, maybe? Or dessert?"

Webb looked at her eager, smiling face, rosy from the cold. She was pretty, he thought. Maxie Gallagher was the prettiest girl he knew, the nicest. She was pretty, she was sweet and thoughtful, but she suddenly seemed like a Barbie doll. He knew that wasn't fair, but still he looked away. "Gosh, I—you know, that sounds great, but I'm coming back here tomorrow to help my mom catch up and, uh, I got that Heathcliff book to finish."

"Wuthering Heights?" She laughed. "Since when were you so conscientious?"

"Yeah, I know," he said, rolling a length of gold drapery cord around his hand. "But I just have to get it done." He could feel Maxie looking at him. "Thanks, though. Really."

"Well," she said uncertainly. She stared at him a moment longer, then turned and hurried down the aisle, her red cape drifting behind her.

By Wednesday afternoon he had figured out what he was going to say to Dylis. He deliberately didn't bring a towel, and when he got off the treadmill he walked over to where she was kneeling on the floor holding Mrs. Wallaker's feet while she did sit-ups.

"Hey, Dylis?"

She looked up in surprise.

"Hi."

Dylis looked back at Mrs. Wallaker. "If you can, go a little slower, work those abs a little harder."

"Yeah," Webb said, bending over, his hands on his knees, "and if you want an even better workout, take your hands from behind your head."

Dylis looked at him. "You want something?"

He nodded. "A towel. Please," he added.

"Over there." She pointed with her head to a chair stacked with white towels.

"Thanks," he said. "I really appreciate it. I was going to bring one from home, but then I remembered how you're always going around passing out towels to everyone like some kind of . . . of towel dispenser." He winced, wishing he had phrased it a little better. Dylis and Mrs. Wallaker were both staring at him, so he limped away.

"You left your crutches in the lobby," she called after him.

He picked up a towel and looked back, smiling. "Thanks." Flinging the towel around his neck, he went over and straddled the leg curl machine, wondering why, when he had been nicer to Dylis than he had ever been in his life, she didn't at least smile back. Listlessly he lifted the weights with his left leg and then lifted fewer weights with his right leg. Back and forth, back and forth, in time to the Napalms singing, " 'Like a blade cutting through my heart, comes the voice, comes the voice, through the stone. . . .' " He watched Dylis out of the corner of his eye. She made the rounds, checking on every single person in the room, handing out towels, giving encouragement, patting Annie on the head like a puppy. But she walked past Webb without a glance. What would it cost her to at least look his way?

A few minutes later, Ken came over. "How's it going, Webb?"

He nodded. "Okay."

"You getting down, Webb?" Ken's one eyebrow furrowed across his forehead. "You sound a little low."

Webb shrugged. "You know."

Ken nodded. "It's always slower than you want it to be, man."

"Yeah." Webb paused. "Hey, could you send Dylis over here? I need to . . . I'd like another towel."

"Sure thing." Ken clapped him on the shoulder. "Take 'er easy."

In a minute Dylis was there holding out a towel.

"Uh, thanks." He took it. She turned away, and he said, "Hey, Dylis?"

"What?" She looked suspicious.

"Well, I just wanted to ask you something." He licked his lips, dabbed at his face with the towel. "Listen, would you do me a favor?"

She put her hands on her hips and stared at him.

He took a deep breath, and words he'd never intended to say tumbled out. "Why don't you like me?"

Her eyes widened, and she gave a snort. "Don't be stupid, Webber. Everyone loves you. Everyone feels sorry for you. Here's Mr. Speedball limping around on one leg. The fastest guy in school gets run over by a *drunk driver*. I want to cry."

He winced. "Dylis."

"And you feel sorrier for yourself than anyone else. Pretty soon everyone is going to forget what a hero you are. They'll just see this poor kid walking around the school with a limp. And then you'll really have something to feel sorry about. But please," she said, pushing back her hair, "don't give a thought to Taffy Putnam. Don't waste a drop of remorse on her."

Webb stared at her. He hadn't meant to ask the question. Dylis's face was flushed, and she was breathing hard. "I—I do," he stammered. "I do feel terrible about what happened. Is that what you mean?" he asked uncertainly.

Dylis just stared at him, stony-faced.

"She . . . your friend . . . didn't deserve that. It was a terrible mistake, that accident. I—I'm sorry it happened to her." He said it again. "I'm sorry." He felt frightened, as if her hard, dark eyes were looking into his soul. "I wish it had happened to me," he went on. "I—I wish I was the one lying in the hospital with all those tubes in me and she was running around free as a bird, riding her bike—"

"Liar," Dylis said through her teeth. "You're so glad it didn't happen to you, that you got off with a broken leg and a few months of therapy. You don't know the first thing about compassion. All you know is how to be cool, how to have a good time. You're heartless."

He bowed his head and stood there while her words fell on him. Finally he glanced up, opened his mouth to say something, but nothing came out. He hung his head again, rubbed his arms up and down. Then he nodded. "Okay," he murmured. "Okay."

Dylis walked away.

Webb got through the rest of the afternoon. He sang along with the piped-in music, hummed along when he didn't know the words, trying to make the hopeless feeling go away, the tightness in his chest.

When he got to the lobby, Dylis followed him. "Your crutches." She handed them over, her face still pinched and red.

He nodded. When she turned to go he called her back. "Listen," he said, "what I said about my grandfather the other day?"

"I know," she said. "It was a lie. Don't worry." She smirked. "I didn't tell my father." She crossed her arms over her chest. "I just wonder what else you lied about."

He stared at her. "What do you mean?"

She walked away.

chapter 15

HE WAS pushing Taffy Putnam on the merry-go-round, running faster and faster, until her eyes grew wide with fear. But even then Webb didn't stop. He didn't stop until Taffy lost her grip and went flying off the merry-go-round.

The dreams kept him from sleeping, and every day he was more exhausted. He had trouble concentrating in his classes. While his English teacher stood in front and droned on about subject, object, direct object, Webb sat in the back and stared at things in the room. He stared at dissected sentences at the top of the blackboard; he stared at a piece of colored string dangling from the overhead light.

"What is it, Webber, about that light that you find so

fascinating? Could you share it with the class?" Mrs. Bragonier said, her voice brassy.

But Webb barely noticed; he barely noticed the giggles of the kids around him when he refocused his gaze on Mrs. Bragonier holding a piece of chalk in the air like she was about to begin conducting a symphony. He had been thinking about his father. When Webb was six or seven he had been standing on the dock, watching some bigger boys fish. There were three of them, maybe five years older than Webb, skinny and loud, shoving each other, dropping worms down each other's shirts. It had been a late spring day, warm, with a breeze that smelled of lilacs. Webb's father had promised to take him out in their little motorboat to fish for bass. Webb was impatient, waiting for his father to get back from his Saturday-morning errands. He wanted to be having as much fun as the bigger boys, talking loudly and showing off.

He stood there for a long time, joining in their laughter from where he waited, down the dock. He watched while they baited their hooks and dropped in their lines off the end of the planking. They each caught several crappies, and when they took the fish off their lines, they let them go. But first they did something Webb had never seen before. They gouged out the fish's eyes with a big silver hook, made them blind before throwing them back in the lake. And they laughed and slapped each other on the back. They looked at

Webb standing there hugging a piling, and he laughed too. It gave him a strange feeling in the bottom of his stomach to watch them blinding the fish, but he laughed anyway. He didn't tell his father until they got out beyond the buoy. His father asked if he was sure, and Webb said he was. His father's tan, smiling face turned red, and the veins in his neck stood out like ropes. He swore loudly, not caring that there were families with children sitting out on their patios eating breakfast. In another instant he restarted the motor and was nosing the boat toward shore. At the dock he climbed out and looped the line around a piling, already yelling.

"What kind of boys are you to entertain yourselves with such cruelty?" He was waving his arms and coming at them where they were huddled together at the end of the dock. One of them was still holding the big silver hook. "How could you purposely cause another creature to suffer? And laugh at what you did? Think, boys, think," he roared, "if you have a brain in your head. How would it feel to be thrown into the world with your eyes ripped out?" He grabbed one of the boys—a skinny blond with a dirty face and wild, frightened eyes.

"Who are you?" he demanded.

The boy swallowed and the color drained from his face. "I didn't do nothin'," he said. "We—We were only fishing."

Webb's father held him by the arm and shook him.

"Liar," he said. "You've got no respect for the fish and no respect for yourselves." He let go of the boy, who shrank back with his buddies against the piling.

They watched openmouthed while Webb's father snapped their cane poles over his knee like toothpicks. "Since you don't know a damn thing about fishing, you won't be needing these." He dropped the broken poles at their feet. "I fear for you boys. I fear for you more than I fear for those poor, bloody fish. You've done something terrible and you don't even own up to it. You're heartless and you're liars." His face was still red with anger, but his voice was quieter, almost sad. "Go on. Get out of here." He pointed their way down the dock to land, and they ran, stumbling over each other.

Now, Webb remembered his father's words: "You've done something terrible and you don't even own up to it. You're heartless and you're liars." It was what Dylis had said about Webb. Was that what he was? He pressed the heels of his hands into his eyes and wished he could crawl under a desk and fall asleep for about ten years. He was tired, so tired. Mrs. Bragonier's voice droned on and on. But he couldn't think about Mrs. Bragonier; he couldn't think about school. All he could think about was what Dylis had said. It was like her words had put a curse on him, like she had some kind of power over him. Whenever he was at the clinic now, he watched her in the mirror so she couldn't sneak up on him. Being on his guard all the time wore him down.

Now he opened his eyes and saw that Maxie was

turned around in her seat staring at him. Webb saw the questions in her eyes. He looked away. He was too tired to think about Maxie.

A beaming, good-natured insurance man from Grampa's auto insurance company came to see them. He said the Putnams were talking about suing. "We've made them an offer," Mr. Hill said. "The most we can go is four hundred thousand." He tapped the coffee table with his pen as he talked.

Grampa nodded, stroking his beard as if considering the amount.

"She was badly injured, you know that," Hill went on, holding the pen between his fingers and rapping it back and forth like a teeter-totter. "She'll never walk again. Hell, she can barely talk." He shook his head. "Terrible loss." Taking a sheaf of papers from his briefcase, he handed them to Grampa, who glanced through them, handed them back. "It's fair," Hill said. "I think it's fair. Whether or not the Putnams will accept . . ." He put the papers back in his briefcase. "They have twenty-eight days to decide. If not, this could go to trial—could be big money in that case—two million, five million." He dropped the pen in his coat pocket, shook Grampa's hand, and was gone, leaving a piney scent of aftershave in the air.

Webb looked across the room at Grampa, who looked as if he was dressed for a funeral in his black suit and gray silk tie. "Where are you going to get four hundred thousand dollars?" he asked.

Grampa ran the knuckles of his hand back and forth under his beard. "Not me," he said. "The insurance company. Aspen Life and Accident—that's what I been paying them for all these years."

Webb heaved a great sigh. "That's great, Grampa. You mean, that's it? The insurance company will cover all the costs? You're off the hook?"

Grampa laughed hollowly. "*If* they settle out of court. *If* they don't sue for punitive damages. *If* they don't take my license away and throw me in jail."

Webb got off the sofa and went over to stand in front of Grampa. "But what do you think? Are they going to settle for that, do you think? Four hundred thousand dollars is a lot of money."

"Phhh. It's a pittance. Four hundred thousand for never walking again, for sitting in her wheelchair looking at TV while all her friends are out playing hopscotch, for never going dancing with her boyfriend. She'll have to sit on the sidelines for the rest of her life, and her family will have to take care of her. There's not enough money in the world," he said morosely.

Webb shoved his hands in his pockets and limped over to the window. It was the beginning of March. Snowing again. The lake was still frozen, still buried under the snow. At the marina the big pilings stood in gray rows like a regiment of soldiers. Once in early

May, he and his father had run out the door in their swimsuits with his mother yelling after them. They ran down to the dock in the noonday sun and dove head-first into the frigid water. "Like jumping into a tray of ice cubes," his father said later. Webb hollered and whooped it up for as long as his father did—about one minute—then scrambled out, shocked by his bravery as much as by the icy water. He lay pressed up next to his father on the dock, trembling, trying to get warm. He could still see his skinny white leg shaking like a dog's tail next to the thick, hairy leg of his father. But he was proud. Not afraid of anything. Like his father.

Grampa came up behind him, put his arms around Webb. " '. . . plunged in the battery-smoke/Right thro' the line they broke;/Cossack and Russian/Reel'd from the sabre-stroke—' "

"What? What, Grampa?" Webb turned around, realizing that he hadn't heard a single word. "Why are you always talking about battles?" he asked irritably. "What difference does it make what happened four hundred years ago or fifty years ago? Who cares? Just drop it."

Grampa stopped talking and looked at Webb for a moment. "You think I'm foolish."

Webb sighed. "I'm sick of hearing about Alexander the Great. I'm sick of hearing about the charge of the Light Brigade. They have nothing to do with me. They're all dead."

Grampa put his arms around Webb again, and Webb felt his beard move up and down against his forehead as he talked. "They may be dead, Boomer, but they're my heroes. They rode into battle, ready to lay down their lives for what they believed in. They may have been afraid, but they tried to do what's right." He stepped back, lifting his chin, and stared at Webb, his eyes shining. "Sometimes the right thing is going into battle against enormous odds. Sometimes it's walking into the valley of death, or maybe, maybe . . ." He wiped his mouth with the back of his hand. "Maybe it's walking out on that ice when every nerve and fiber in your body tells you it's the wrong thing to do but there's a man drowning and you gotta try, you gotta at least try." He took a deep breath. "I gotta do this, Boomer. Even if they send me to jail."

"Don't talk about it anymore!" Webb snapped. "If you want to be such a big hero, why are you always reminding me of what you're doing? You want me to be grateful? To fall on my knees and kiss your feet?"

"No, Boomer—"

Anger rose up in Webb like a tidal wave. "I'll tell you something, Grampa," he snarled. "I'm not that grateful. You didn't save me from anything worse than what I'm going through. I hate my life. My life is crap. All I think about is Taffy Putnam, Taffy Putnam, Taffy Putnam. There's this little kid out there somewhere who'll never walk again. She'll never ride her bike, never go to her prom. And it's my fault." He made a fist and struck his chest. "I was driving the damn car, not you, and you can't pretend that away, not if you go to jail for two hundred years." He snorted. "I might as well be in jail myself—I can't sleep, I can't enjoy my friends. I can't even do my exercises anymore. What's the difference if I can't run anymore? Taffy Putnam can't even walk. I might as well call up the police and confess."

"No!" Grampa cried, grabbing him by the shoulders and giving him a shake. "You're talking nonsense now, Webber. Don't cave in to this. We have to see this through the way we planned. Think—think what this would mean if it fell on your shoulders. Why, not only would you never drive again, but what if they go after more than the four hundred thousand? You know who would pay? Not you—you don't have any money. It's your mother, that's who. For the rest of her life. Do you want to do that to your mother?"

Webb stared at him. "She doesn't have anything to do with this."

"That's how it would be." Grampa put his hand across his chest. "I haven't lived such a good life, Boomer. I wasn't the greatest father. And your grand-mother—God rest her soul—didn't deserve a husband like me. I didn't even go off to fight in the war when every one of my buddies did. But I can do this one thing. Your father would want me to save you and your mother. I know he would." Grampa gave his shoulders another shake. "Boomer?"

Webb looked at Grampa's flushed face. "Yeah," he said wearily. "Okay, Grampa."

chapter 16

WEBB NO longer did his exercises at home. It all seemed pointless to him. His leg wasn't getting any stronger, he wasn't walking any better. If he walked with a limp for the rest of his life, he didn't care.

March dragged along, gray and relentlessly cold. In the evenings after work or after therapy, he walked around the lake alone. He knew that if he asked, Maxie would walk with him, but he didn't want Maxie beside him. He didn't want anyone beside him. If someone came out on their back porch to look at the lake, Webb turned away. He hated the small talk, the exchange of pleasantries people forced on him: "Cold enough for you?" "Take a look at those stars tonight." "More snow tomorrow, the weatherman says." Who cared about the cold? Who cared what the weatherman said? He walked along the shore with his head down, watching his feet. Sometimes he watched his feet break right through a skiff of ice, soaking his tennis shoes. His feet got cold, very cold, but he didn't stop walking. I'm walking through water, he would think, and my feet are getting wet. But it was like he was watching someone else. He barely felt the cold.

He would come back to the warm house, where his mother and Grampa were drinking coffee in front of the television, and he would watch them both jump up to do something for him—get him hot chocolate, cookies, dry socks. Grampa always wanted to rub his cold feet, but Webb didn't want that; he didn't want anything. There was an expression on Grampa's face now that Webb couldn't name. His face was droopy, his eyes pools of sadness. Webb knew he was worried about something. Then he remembered. He was worried about going to jail. But Webb couldn't stop to console him. He watched himself drop his jacket on the chair and continue down the hall to his room, where he had work to do.

He made himself sit at his small brown desk with all the nicks and dents across the top and pick up his books. He knew, in a way, he was being foolish, but he made himself read all the titles of all the books on his desk, not just read them but say them out loud. *"Introduction to Algebra,"* he said, *"Webster's New Collegiate Dictionary, United States Government, This Planet Earth,*

Points of View, Wuthering Heights. Wuthering Heights," he said again, listening to his voice. He sounded far away. Like he was down in a well. But I'm sitting right here, he thought, looking at my hands holding this book. He knew he was acting strange, talking to himself, watching himself. And he felt strange. Like he wasn't inside his body anymore. His body was going along, doing things, eating, reading, talking, and he was standing on the sidelines watching. He had never felt so strange. But he didn't care.

Every Monday, Wednesday, and Friday, Grampa drove him to therapy. Ride the exercise bike, walk the treadmill, squats, the leg-flexing machine, the Biodex machine. Nothing changed. Every week, Ken made him stand on the scales.

"Hey, look at that," he'd say, pointing at the scale. "You're at seventy-five percent. Way to go, man."

Like he'd done something wonderful, Webb thought. When, in fact, he was barely making any progress.

"You keep coming in here without your crutches," Ken scolded. "You still need them, Webb. That leg still needs support. Even though you're doing really well," he added, slapping Webb on the back.

He was trying to pump Webb up, but Webb was like a bicycle tire that had gone flat too many times. He was just going along, doing the things he had always done. Just because he didn't know what else to do. He limped along on the treadmill until someone came by and told him to get off. Sometimes he looked up and saw the boy in the mirror, limping along on that rubber track that wouldn't stop, and he felt sorry for him. He wished the machine would stop so the boy could rest for a little while.

Other times he rode the exercise bike slowly, languorously, and he was a little kid again. The sun was warm on his cheeks, and his T-shirt stuck to his sweaty back as he pedaled up Christmas Tree Hill. It wasn't a steep hill, but a long, gentle incline, and the tree at the top could be seen for miles—a huge, perfect fir with its shaggy top pointing at the sun.

He rode up the hill every day that summer, with a peanut butter sandwich and a chocolate milk in his basket. And Whit Iggins would be there, and Peter Pocknis and Les Russell and Beefy. And before they could eat their sandwiches, they would all sit cross-legged around the tree and chant together: "Issey firkus to biffo, doodle, doodle doo." It was a secret pledge in a secret code to root out evil in the town and the entire countryside. Then they would all break off little pieces of their sandwiches as a sacrifice to the great tree and throw them over their shoulders. After that they would eat as fast as they could so they could wrestle each other down the hill or tell stupid jokes or chase each other into the woods and hide.

He hadn't thought of that summer in a long time, but suddenly, now, he could remember it like it was yesterday. He could smell the pungent, pine-scented ground beneath him, feel the sharpness of the needles as they stuck to his sweaty palms. The heat, the shimmering, piney hot air filled his lungs again as he pedaled around and around on the exercise bike with his eyes closed. He thought how magical it was to be young again, to run without pain, to be carefree. He pedaled on and on, listening to the *thonk, thonk* of a woodpecker in the forest, to the laughter of five boys, to the sweet soughing of the wind in the trees.

"Webber!"

He opened his eyes and looked into Dylis Clark's scowling face. "Huh?"

"I said, 'Do you want a towel?' "

He sighed deeply, reached over and took one. "Thank you," he murmured.

She stood there for a moment. "What's with you?"

Webb looked back at her, at her eyes like dark cinders peering out from under the bush of dark hair, her plain white face with its hard little mouth. Dylis didn't like him, he knew that. But with her, he felt something. He felt real, like he really existed. It wasn't a happy feeling. It was a piercing, painful feeling. But at least he felt alive. He didn't know what it was, but Dylis was the only one who made him feel anything at all. "I can't do this anymore," he said to her.

"Yeah, well, get off and let someone else use it. You've been on that thing for twenty minutes."

Webb nodded and got off the bicycle. He stood there for a second, feeling a little wobbly, like he was getting his land legs back after being on a boat.

Dylis put her hands on her hips and regarded him suspiciously. "Are you just going to stand there? You've got thirty minutes left."

"Dylis," he said, looking at his feet. "I don't know what to do."

"Well, don't ask me," she said, turning away. "I'm just the towel dispenser."

"Wait!"

Dylis turned back, rolling her eyes.

"Tell me something." He was asking for it. He knew he was asking for trouble. But he couldn't help himself. The words tumbled out. "Tell me about Taffy. Tell me how she is."

Dylis's eyes widened, and she gave him an incredulous smile. "What? You, Webber Freegy, actually showing some concern? Am I hearing things?"

"Listen," he said slowly, trying to pick his words with care, "I am concerned. I really want to know."

"She's terrible. You know that," she said angrily. "She's a mess."

"Specifically," he said carefully, afraid to look at Dylis, afraid to rouse her fury. "Tell me specifically. Can she—Can she use her legs?"

"No," Dylis said sharply. "No, she can't use her legs. She'll probably never use her legs again. She'll be in a wheelchair for the next seventy-five years. Until she dies, thanks to—"

Webb lifted his eyes from the floor and stared at her.

"Your grandfather," she said hotly.

186

Webb took a breath but couldn't get enough air because of the heaviness in his chest. He opened his mouth and tried again, conscious of Dylis's anger like a forest fire raging around him. "Well," he said, trying again, "can she, ah . . . don't get mad, Dylis, I just need to know this. Can she talk?"

"What's your point?" Dylis snapped. "Just what kind of case are you building here, Webber? I know it has something to do with the cheesy settlement they offered her. Like that's going to fix everything. Well, you know what you can do with your money—you and your grandfather and the insurance company. You can all just build yourself a big bonfire and roast in it."

"Wait—" Webb said, but she marched off.

He stood there with his hand out. With every fiber of his being he wanted her to come back and talk to him. When Dylis was next to him, he felt her rage like a current of electricity running from her into him. She didn't race around fixing him hot chocolate, offering to rub his feet, buying him key chains. She saw into him, saw the blackness of his soul. He was who he was with Dylis. He didn't have to pretend with her. He stood there watching her spray the mirror on the opposite wall and rub it until it gleamed. Every once in a while, she would call out words of encouragement to Al and Annie. Dylis was right. Four hundred thousand dollars was not enough for Taffy. He needed to tell Dylis that.

He limped across the gray carpeting, watching Dylis in the mirror. She would try to get away from him, but

he wouldn't let her. He had to find out about Taffy
Putnam. That was the only thing that mattered anymore. Somehow he knew that Taffy Putnam's fate was
his fate. Why should he ever speak again if she couldn't
talk? Why should he take another bit of food if she
couldn't eat? Maybe she would have feeding tubes in
her for the rest of her life, like he'd had in the hospital.
He thought with sharp longing of his weeks in the
hospital, of his incapacity. He would choose that,
choose the pain, choose not being able to walk or talk
or eat, rather than this. The blank nothingness of his
brain had been so easy. Having no memory was a gift, a
treasure.

"Dylis!" He called across the floor, and she put down
her spray bottle, the roll of paper towels, and folded her
arms over her chest, waiting for his slow progress across
the room.

"I only want to know how she's doing," he said
breathlessly. "I care about her. I think about her all—I
think about her a lot."

Dylis nodded. "Very touching. I'll tell her. It'll cheer
her right up. It'll be the nicest thing that's happened to
her since the bowl of cream of wheat she had for dinner
last night."

She was eating! Even if it was only creamed cereal. It
was a little hope. "Tell her," he said eagerly, "tell her,
tell her when she . . ." He had an idea forming, one
that suddenly lifted his spirits, of something he could do
for Taffy. "When she gets strong enough, I'll—I'll, tell

her Webber, the guy in the car—" He stopped. What was it he could give this little girl? Nothing. Nothing in the world would change what he had done. "Forget it," he said, sagging back down into himself. "It was a dumb idea." He limped back across the floor to wait for Grampa.

chapter 17

IT WAS St. Patrick's Day. Everyone at school wore green, even the teachers, even the kids who weren't Irish. On the public address, after the announcements, they played "When Irish Eyes Are Smiling." The principal, Mr. O'Brady, played it every year. The kids in Webb's homeroom laughed and cheered. Webb tried to join in because everyone else was, but he didn't care if they played "Jingle Bells." He wasn't wearing green. He didn't even know what day it was.

Maxie caught up with him on the way out the door. "Web-ber," she said in a scolding voice. "You don't have any green on. Let me see your socks." She lifted his pants leg and shook her head. "White socks—you're hopeless."

Webb looked at her. She was wearing a green sweater and skirt and a matching green ribbon in her hair. He knew he was a disappointment to Maxie these days. He didn't wait for her at his locker anymore. He didn't walk to the cafeteria with her. Or call her. Now he had forgotten to wear green. He wanted to tell her how silly she was for making such a big deal about green clothes. But he wasn't sure. Maybe it was more important than he thought. Everyone, almost everyone in school, was wearing green. Even Mr. Wolski had a green hanky tucked in his pocket. Maybe Webb was the one who was being silly. Maybe everyone was talking about him because he was wearing a gray sweatshirt and jeans. "I'm sorry," he muttered. Then, to get away from her, he said, "I've got to get going. I've got to see Beefy about something."

All the cheeriness went out of Maxie's face. She looked like she was going to cry. But Webb couldn't help himself. He couldn't think of anything to say to her anymore. He knew he used to talk with her a lot, but it almost seemed like it was someone else walking her around in the hallways. Maxie's boyfriend, everyone called him. But now he knew he didn't belong with Maxie. She belonged with someone who liked to laugh, who liked to have fun. Not him.

With Beefy it was better. Beefy said, "Hey, man, how's it going?" And Webb didn't have to say one thing. He didn't even have to fake a smile. He just walked down the hallway and watched Beefy high-five everyone. In the cafeteria, though, Beefy said something that worried Webb. "Whatsa matter?" he asked, putting his sandwich down on the table and leaning forward to look into Webb's face. "I asked you three times, Spider Webb, whether you were going to Covault's party this weekend. And you're off in La La Land. What's bugging you, man? Why are you acting so weird?"

Webb forced himself to focus on Beefy. He looked at his green-and-white-striped shirt with the mustard stain in the shape of a fish. He looked at Beefy's round red face, the brown freckles across his round red nose, his blue eyes with their pale fringe of eyelashes. "What do you mean?" he asked, concentrating on paying attention to Beefy and what came out of his mouth.

"You're acting goofy," Beefy said. "Like you're a million miles away."

"I am?" Webb looked down at his gray sweatshirt, his hands with the bitten-off fingernails, holding a ham sandwich on wheat bread. I'm right here, he thought, sitting in the cafeteria eating my sandwich. "I'm tired," he finally said.

"Well, get some sleep," Beefy snapped, going back to his lunch.

Webb knew there was something wrong with him. He didn't feel like himself. He didn't even know who himself was. He tried to concentrate in his classes, but he *was* a million miles away, watching Webber sitting at

a little oak desk in his gray sweatshirt, watching Mrs.
Bragonier write "scavengers of the eastern seaboard" on
the blackboard. It didn't make any sense. He would
think about it after school, he decided. He didn't have
to work or go to therapy. There would be time for
thinking.

When he got off the bus, Webb didn't cross the street
to his house. Grampa would be there, and Grampa always confused things. He needed to think this out by
himself. He walked farther down and crossed over to
the marina, where the big gray dock stood deserted in
the late-afternoon sun. There was a cold wind that
stung his ears as he walked around to the back of the
little shed where he often sat in the summertime, taking
people's money, helping them launch their boats or
pumping gas. He didn't think he would do that anymore. Not this summer. At the back of the shed there
were a couple of small overturned fishing boats that
belonged to Marty, the owner of the marina. Webb sat
down on one of the hulls and leaned back against the
shed, adjusting the books in his backpack to get comfortable. He sat there for a long time, out of the wind,
watching the lake. It had stayed frozen longer this year
than any year he could remember. It was the middle of
March and it hadn't come apart yet. But all the snow
was gone; the fishing shanties were gone, dragged back
across the ice and stowed behind garages for another

year. It wouldn't be that long. Still, there were no deep cracks, only a fine web of dark lines over the gray ice. Web, he thought. Like himself spread over the ice.

He shook his head. This wasn't what he came to think about. He came to think about his life, about why he was feeling so strange. He thought back to the accident, about waking up in the green hospital room. That was when his life began to change. It was having a broken leg, not being able to run anymore. He closed his eyes and imagined himself running down Scott Street, his face in the sun, knees high. He could hear his breath in his ears, small, steady puffs, warm under his nose, the drum of his feet against the pavement, the hot, greasy smell of fries as he passed Porky's Diner. But mostly he felt the strength of his body, the sureness of his legs that could carry him anywhere. That was what he missed.

He shook his head again. "You're a damn liar, Webb," he said out loud to himself. It wasn't that at all. He opened his eyes and looked out over the ice. There, hanging over the lake, was the face of Taffy Putnam, her eyes as wide as two saucers, staring at him. That was it. He had ruined her life. Everyone in the world felt sorry for him because they didn't know better. They should hate him. He ran over her and then lied about it. He was a liar. Heartless. And everyone felt sorry for him because he couldn't run anymore. That was the funny thing. They bought him presents and hugged him and high-fived him and waited on him and admired him. Because they didn't know what he had done to Taffy Putnam.

And he couldn't tell anyone the truth, couldn't tell even his mother the truth. Because then they would send him to jail. And his mother would have to support Taffy Putnam for the rest of her life. She would have to sew drapes for all the windows of all the houses in Lemon Lake, and even that wouldn't be enough. She would be ruined. And it would be his fault. His father would never forgive him for that.

That was it, then, Webb thought. He used to be one thing, and now he was something else. And he could never go back. He stood up slowly, wincing at the pain in his leg. He started forward, down the hill toward the big dock, taking baby steps because the snow had crusted and become icy. And because of his bad leg. His footsteps made dozens of crunching sounds as he moved down the hill sideways to keep from sliding. When he got to the dock, he was actually tired, like he had run in a big race. Away from the building the wind bit at his face. He grabbed hold of the piling to steady himself, to rest. After a few minutes, he walked forward along the dock, into the wind.

There was something about the lake that always drew him, summer or winter. Maybe it was because his mother had forbidden him to go out on the lake alone. Even in the middle of January, when there was no danger, she wouldn't let him go out. Every winter it rankled him that he couldn't walk out there and just cut a hole in the ice and drop in a line. But he had promised.

He stood now at the end of the pier and looked off to his left, out from the shore about two hundred yards. He lined his sight up with a yellow garage that had a sunflower painted on the back. You couldn't see it from the shore, but when you were out in a boat you could see that big, stupid sunflower. Or when you were just out standing on the ice. He picked a spot on the ice about two hundred yards out from the garage. That was the spot. He remembered everything.

It was a Saturday morning in early March, almost lunchtime, but he and his father were cooking a late breakfast because they had been out of eggs, and when they were leaving to get the eggs his mother had given them a long grocery list and they didn't get back until eleven. His mother was in her sewing room, trying to finish a dress she was wearing to a wedding. Webb's cousin Doreen was getting married. Webb was invited too, and he was sitting on a stool making toast while his father told him what to expect.

"First," his father said, cracking the seventh egg into the blue omelette bowl, "is the ceremony at the church. Doreen goes down the aisle with Uncle Johnny and Uncle Johnny turns her over to Jason, the guy she's going to marry."

"The guy with the apple in his neck?" Webb wanted to know.

"The Adam's apple, right," his father said, pouring the eggs into a sizzling pan on the stove. "Then the priest says, 'Do you take this woman for your wife; do you take this man for your husband? Do you promise to take her out dancing every Saturday night; do you promise to fix him breakfast in bed on his birthday?' and so forth. And they say, 'I do, I do,' and they kiss each other, and that's it."

"That's it?" Webber wailed. "What about the cake and ice cream and the big party with everybody dancing?"

"That's the second part," his father said. He turned off the stove. "You can stop making toast now. You've got enough for an army, plus the twelve ducks in the front yard." He glanced out the window. "Man, I don't know what that guy thinks he's doing, going out on the ice," he said, leaning toward the window and looking to his left. "Only thing he's going to catch is wet feet. Guy ought to know better after that thaw last week. The lake is already coming apart in spots. All right, Webb, go get your mother. This is just about done. First set the table."

His father got the orange juice out of the refrigerator and poured out three glasses, then glanced back out the window. "My God!" he yelled, slamming down the pitcher of juice so that it slopped up over the sides and onto the red-and-white-checked tablecloth. He looked at Webb, his eyes dark and angry. "He's gone in. Tell Mom—call nine-one-one."

His father grabbed his jacket, pulling it on as he went, and flew out the door. "Wait!" Webb cried. "I want to go too." He wanted his father to take him, to let him be part of the excitement, whatever it was. He climbed up on the counter and kneeled there watching his father run down the south shore, his red-and-black-plaid jacket flying out behind him.

"Mom!" Webb climbed down and raced into the sewing room, where his mother was bent over a red dress with pins in her mouth. "A man!" Webb pointed. "He fell through the ice and Dad is—"

"Oh, no." She jumped up, the pins falling from her lips; she already knew before Webb could tell her. "Oh, no, Webber. Which way did he go?"

He knew then; Webb knew that he wasn't going to miss out on the excitement after all, because he could go with his mother to see the man floundering in the icy water. To watch his father pull him out. He danced around while his mother made the call and then, like his father, dashed out the door, pulling on his jacket.

They ran, he and his mother, out into the snowy yard, past the quacking ducks to the frozen shoreline. As they ran they could see the man moving up and down in the hole, grabbing for a hold, over and over. He was wearing a red hat. But they couldn't see his father. Not yet. They ran past the Strobels' house, which was hidden by frozen sheets pinned to the line and swaying back and forth like pink boards in the breeze. But Mrs.

Strobel was out there in her husband's galoshes, round-ing up her cats.

"Someone's gone through the ice," his mother cried as they ran by. "D. went out to help."

Webb raced ahead of his mother, leaping overturned boats, leaping brown bushes. The police would be there. He might get his picture in the paper. It was still exciting when he got to the yellow garage and saw that his father had gone out on the ice. He wanted to tell his mother to stop yelling for his father to come back. His father could do anything. He could ski down a hill backward; he could dive off the highest board; and he could swim across the lake three times in a row. He could break his leg and crawl through the woods for half a mile and not even cry.

Other people came out of their houses and stood beside Webb and his mom, and they talked about what should be done.

"He's got a rope," someone said. "See it dangling down on the ice?"

"That's not the way," another man said. "He should have a ladder, see, shove it out there to stabilize the ice, displace the weight."

But nobody else went out there on the creaky, gray ice. They all stood on the shore, hugging themselves, watching the big man in the black-and-red jacket inch-ing his way forward, slowly but without fear. He never looked back. They could see him talking to the man, who was quieter now, not grabbing and yelling but dazed-looking, clinging to the ice around him like he was part of it. Like he was frozen into it already.

His father stretched himself out on the ice, threw the line with a loop at the end, and yelled at the man, giving him directions. Webb heard him say, "Nice and easy, don't worry." It took him three tries, but the man got the loop over his head. Webb's dad pulled and yelled, especially when the ice kept breaking around the man. "Don't give up," he yelled. He yelled that over and over, even though it looked like the man would never get out of the hole. "Don't give up."

Slowly, as slowly as snow melts, the man rose up a little bit on the ice. He laid his cheek against the frozen lake. It looked like he would never move again. But it was enough. His dad pulled him forward one inch at a time like a giant fish that he had played out in the water. The man wiggled a little, trying to help, until his whole trunk was on the ice and, finally, his wet black legs.

The crowd of people onshore, who had been holding their breath, cheered. Webb, who was caught in his mother's grip, cheered loudest of all. His father was still yelling at the man, who couldn't stand up, urging him to move forward, to crawl to shore, to not just lie there. And the man crawled across the ice like a wounded bear, the rope still around his belly, too weary to even raise his head and see all the people cheering for him. Even Webb was looking at the man when his father went through the ice. He didn't even see him go. His mother screamed and squeezed Webb tighter. "D.!" she yelled. "Somebody help him!"

"Help him! Help him!" she kept yelling as the police, the ambulance, and the fire truck all roared in. She yelled more than Webb had ever heard her yell before. After they pulled Jack Asbury to safety and went out for Webb's father, the people stood silently and watched, certain that with all the rescuers and equipment, he would be brought back quickly. Only his mother wasn't silent. "D.," she cried, over and over, like a peeping bird. They watched the hole for ten minutes, fifteen minutes, watched the firemen in rubber suits ease themselves down, one after another, into the hole.

"He'll be okay," Webb kept saying. "I know he'll come back up, Mom." He believed it for eight more days. He believed that his father had gone under the ice and found a way out on the other side of the lake and he would surprise them and show up for dinner one night, saying something like "Well, if you had baked walleye for dinner last Tuesday, I would have come home sooner." Then they found his body and Webb couldn't fool himself anymore.

Now Webb stared out at the lake, at the spot where he last saw his father—stretched out on the ice in his black-and-red jacket, saying his last words to someone he didn't even know. A second later he was gone. Webb thought about being in the icy darkness, running out of air, that terrible burning in your chest after you've run your guts out and you can't get enough air. Only worse.

He squeezed his eyes shut and took a deep breath. But maybe, he thought, opening his eyes and looking out at the lake again, maybe his father hadn't been all that scared. Maybe he'd been certain he was going to find that hole and bob right up again into the faces of all the rescuers. He must have heard the sirens. Maybe he'd just been thinking about going back to the warm house, eating a nice, warm omelette. Maybe he'd thought, My boy, my boy, I've got to get home to my boy.

Webb sighed, shivering in his canvas jacket, not taking his eyes from the spot. It was like a grave, he thought—the place where his father was buried. He had taken flowers out to the cemetery with his mother, but he had never taken anything to that spot. His father had lain under there for eight days. Webb sat down on the edge of the pier, and, holding one of the pilings, he eased himself down onto the ice.

chapter 18

WEBB WALKED gingerly, favoring his right leg. Under his tennis shoes the ice was slippery. If he had given it any thought, he would have been wearing his lug-soled boots. But if he went back for them now, he would probably change his mind.

As he inched forward he could feel the cold rise up from the ice and penetrate his right leg. But he didn't mind that. He didn't mind the pain in his leg anymore. It had become like an old friend. Sometimes it seemed like the pain in his leg was the only old friend he had, he thought as he pulled up his collar against the wind. Beefy, Maxie—they were gone from his life somehow. Even Grampa. The accident had pulled them right apart, so far apart they didn't even know each other anymore. Grampa was trying to save his life, and it didn't matter. The truth was, there wasn't much to save anymore. Webb had no friends, nothing he liked to do—he wouldn't run if he could. He didn't even like the taste of his food anymore. The truth was, he thought, there was no truth.

He stopped, looking around. He was out far enough. Down the lake another hundred yards, he could see the yellow garage. In front of him he spotted a round dark spot in the ice where a fishing hole had been, and he skirted it. His mother always told him he wasn't careful enough, but look, he thought, look how careful he was being, testing every step, watching for fishing holes. She wouldn't like this, though, he thought regretfully. He had promised her he wouldn't come out on the lake alone. Especially now, in March. She would get mad at him for this. He was breaking a promise to his mother, but it seemed like he had to. It was the only thing he had had to do for a long time.

After he got past the hole, he heard a dog barking and he stopped. Just even with him there was a setter racing back and forth on the shore. The setter belonged to a family who lived in a black cabin down the lake. The dog's name was Red, and he was always loose, running through people's flowers, crapping in their yards. Lots of times he would come from out of nowhere when Webb was running and run alongside him. Just as if he belonged to Webb. Webb would say, "Come on, Red, let's pour it on these last two miles." And Red would pick up his pace without even trying. And when Webb collapsed in the grass at the end, Red would run around him in circles and lick his sweaty face. But Webb hadn't seen him in five months, since he'd stopped running. He wondered if the dog would come to him. "Red!" he called.

The dog's ears pricked up. He stopped barking.

"Red!" Webb whistled.

Red stood like a statue and looked out at the lake.

"C'mon, boy."

The dog inched closer to the shoreline but then stopped. He looked at Webb for a moment, then turned and ran the other way, disappearing behind a stand of evergreens.

Webb shrugged and started walking down the lake again. Seeing Red had stirred his feelings for just a second. It was the memory of who he used to be. Now he felt flat again, not even disappointed that the dog didn't remember him. He himself barely remembered who he used to be. Red had never seen him limping. Maybe he thought it was an old man out there on the ice. Never mind, Webb thought. It wasn't important.

He stopped when he got to the place on the ice where he was opposite the sunflower on the garage. Two hundred yards from shore. Yes, Webb thought, looking down. This was the spot. He struck it lightly with his heel as if marking it. Then he stood over it silently and tried to think of something to say. *Half a league, half a league,/Half a league onward . . . /Into the valley of Death/Rode the six hundred.* He shook his head, trying to clear it. If he could just remember a prayer or something. *Our Father who art in heaven . . .* He had stopped going to Mass because his mother didn't make him go anymore after his father died. He put his hands in his pockets and took a deep breath. " 'Our Father . . . ,' " he said out loud. He waited for more words to come to him. He had walked all the way out here to pay his respects and now he couldn't even think of the right words.

He tried to recall the funeral and the words the priest had used. But Webb had paid no attention to the priest or to the shiny gray coffin covered in flowers. He had busied himself counting the pieces of colored glass in the David and Goliath window next to the pew where they sat. Remembering, he felt ashamed.

Why had he been such a little jerk? At his own father's funeral. Running around eating cake afterward like he was at a birthday party. And he was worse at Fatty's Funland, whooping it up, riding the roller coaster like he was the happiest kid on the planet. Webb lifted his head and looked around at the lake, at the houses with all their lights on, people coming home from work, making dinner. "Geez," he said, plowing his hands through his hair. "What am I doing here?"

He should get back. Grampa would be worrying. But still he stood there. He didn't feel anything for anybody, but he thought maybe here, out here on the lake, there would be something, a connection.

"What a saphead," he said into the wind. "I've always been a stupid saphead. Faking it, always faking it. Now I screwed up royally. I screwed up so bad I can't get unscrewed. I don't know, Dad, what I'm doing anymore. I did that awful thing—" He stopped. A vision rose up out of the ice—a small white mask of fear, braids flying, her mouth open in a soundless scream. He wanted to scream back, to fall to his knees, to close his eyes, to close all his senses so he would never see her again, never feel what he was feeling again. Tears burned in his throat and welled up in his eyes. But he kept going, kept talking to his father. "You know," he said hoarsely, "you know what I did." He clenched his fists and held them against his chest. "And then I lied about it. And I lied and I lied and I lied. I don't even know who I am anymore, I told the lie so many times."

He stopped and breathed slowly in and out until the vision left him. He looked across the lake, where a flock of geese was flying low over Marshbank Park. He waited till they had all landed on the ice before he started talking again. "You want to know something?" He snuffled loudly and stopped to wipe his nose on his jacket sleeve. "I'd rather be in the wheelchair the rest of my life if I could undo what I did to her. She's just a little kid who didn't do anything. God, I feel so bad." He shivered, feeling the cold right through his jacket to the middle of his stomach. "I feel so bad, sometimes I'd rather be dead."

His leg ached like someone had hit it with a baseball

bat. He went on. "I think about you telling me to always do my best, to be generous, to tell the truth, even over small things like a dime or something. I hated it, like when you made me tell Mrs. Wade I cut up her floor with my ice skates—stuff like that." Webb tried to laugh, but it came out like a sob. "Dad?" He bit his lip. "Why did you leave me?"

He was so cold now, his teeth were chattering. "Wh-Where are you, Dad? Help me. Why don't you help me?" He hung his head and stood there silently, absorbing the cold around him, beneath him, taking it into his bones, into his blood, with a kind of resignation. Finally he raised his head. "I don't know why I came out here." He looked back toward home.

He turned and took a step back the way he had come. He could barely move, he was so stiff with the cold. The sun was sitting like a white ball on the roof of somebody's house over on the west shore. Slowly he bent one knee back and forth, then the other, did a windmill with one arm, then the other. He took another step. Then he remembered. He wanted to lay something there—a flower or a ribbon. A little marker. He looked around on the ice. Nothing but some wind-blown twigs, clumps of snow. He felt in the pockets of his jacket and pulled out a used handkerchief and a bone-colored wooden button. He looked at the button. It had come off his jacket back in October, and he'd been carrying it around for five months. It was all he had. He bent down and set it on the ice. When he stood up he could hardly see it. He thought of something else. Taking off his backpack, he rummaged in it until he found his mechanical pencil. He got down on his left knee, jabbed at the ice, and poked a little hole. He jabbed again and again and again, feeling the chips fly up against his frozen hand.

Suddenly the ice cracked under his knee. In a flash, he shoved himself away, a wave of hot fear racing through his chest. "What the hell are you doing, Webber?" he said out loud. Another instant and the ice would have given way underneath him. Even in that brief moment the water had sprung up through the crack and wet his knee. He felt the numbing cold there worse than anywhere now. He should get off the ice. But suddenly what he was doing was more important than warmth, more important than feeling safe. He had to finish the hole. He pushed himself around to the other side of the hole on his belly and jabbed and jabbed at the ice until the hole was big enough. He reached back in his pocket and dropped the button in. It floated—a small boat in a dark little pond.

He slid back from the hole and sat up, watching the button floating in the lake. Now he could go back. He had left a marker, a memento for his father. He looked again at the lights on the shore, brighter now against the fading sky. He knew it was warmer there, but still he wasn't ready to leave. Here, on the lake, he was alone with his father; nothing of that other world could touch him. He felt almost peaceful. He thought of his mother—how upset she would be if she got home from work and he wasn't there. If she knew he had come out here after all his promises. And Grampa, who would somehow blame himself if anything happened to him. But so what? No, he wasn't ready to go back yet. He watched the little hole of dark water cradle the button.

He wondered how his father felt when he went through the ice, when he hit that frigid water and sank. When he figured out that he wasn't ever going to come back up again. Did he think what a stupid thing it was that he had done, coming out to save someone so dim-witted that he didn't know enough to stay off the ice when it was so soft? Did he wish, in those few minutes, that he could do it over, that he could just stand on shore and wring his hands with the other people? And then go home with his wife and son to eat his breakfast? While everyone thought he was such a hero, maybe he was feeling like a stupid saphead. But it was too late by then.

"I should have done it differently," Webb said. Out on the windswept lake there was only his father to hear. "After it happened I didn't want people blaming me. I didn't want to go to jail. I wanted to just keep going along, going out with my friends, getting back to running." He sighed heavily. "Maybe I know what you felt like when you were drowning. Maybe you wish you had done it differently too. Maybe you wish you had waited for the fire trucks. But it was too late."

Webb watched the little pool of water gather the orange and pink colors of the sunset, and with the changing light, the water seemed to spread around him, across the lake. And he felt like he was lifted up by the water, floating gently away in a never-ceasing current. He looked over in time to see the geese take off in one great noisy sweep. He uncurled himself, stretched out on the ice, and laid his cheek next to the hole. It came to him then that his father had done the right thing, that he would do it all the same way again. Given the chance. But who gets second chances after they're dead? Unless you're walking around dead.

Webb lay there. The terrible cold was like a blanket of ice over his body, numbing his fingers, his toes, thickening his blood. But in his leg, deep in the bone, the small pulse of pain went on and on. He stood up. He started back to shore.

chapter 19

HE KNEW where they lived. On the corner of Pacific and Jones, her father had said. When he got there he found a house on each corner. Two had lights on inside. Only one had a dolphin painted on the mailbox. Webb started up the walk, breathing deeply, trying to quiet the beating of his heart.

Dylis opened the door. She looked behind him as if the explanation for his being there lay beyond him, down the sidewalk. She looked back at Webb. "What do you want?"

Webb swallowed. "I need to . . . to talk to . . . Is your father here?"

"What do you want?" She crossed her arms over her chest.

"Look, Dylis, all I'm asking . . ." He stopped. Her father appeared in the doorway behind her, dressed in civilian clothes.

"Webber, this is a surprise. Isn't it, Dylis?" He looked down at her, smiling a little, and pushed her gently out of the way to open the door. "C'mon in."

Webb stepped into a small, cluttered living room. Two TV trays with dinners on them were set up in front of a giant aquarium full of colored fish. "Oh—um," Webb stammered, "you're eating. I—This will be quick. I don't even have to sit down."

"We *were* eating," Dylis said, not softening her tone.

Her father gave her a look. He pushed Webb forward into the room. "Dinner can wait. It looks like you have something on your mind." He motioned for Webb to sit in a chair, while he sat opposite him on a brown plaid sofa. Dylis sat beside her father. She picked up a pillow and held it against her, not taking her eyes from Webb's face.

Her father glanced at her. "You want to eat, Dylis? Go eat."

Webb shook his head. "No, I want her to stay. She's, she's . . ." He realized that he wanted to tell this to Dylis more than he wanted to tell her father. He cracked his knuckles, aware of the soft bubbling of the fish tank, a gray cat lying along the back of the sofa, staring at him. He could smell their dinners—something spicy with tomato sauce. Spaghetti, he thought, trying to calm himself.

Dylis cleared her throat impatiently, and he looked at her. "I don't know what this will mean," he began, "what will happen to me or my mother because of it, or to my grandfather. But . . ." He drew in a deep, shuddering breath, his heart pounding, and looked down at the gray carpet. "I was driving that day. I was the one who hit Taffy Putnam."

"You?" Dylis struck the pillow with both hands. "You?" her voice shrilled.

Officer Clark stared at Webb, leaning forward on the sofa, his arms resting on his knees. He said nothing. Webb could hear him breathing.

"All this time," Dylis squealed. "All this time you—" Her father put his hand on her knee and she shut up. But she groaned like she was in pain. She threw the pillow on the floor and kicked it.

Webb knew she was trying not to explode. But inside himself he felt something break free. Suddenly the great, beating whirlwind inside him stopped. He felt a great calm settle over him like a blanket. For a moment he closed his eyes and let himself feel it, easy and peaceful, as if he had just awakened from a long sleep. He had told the truth at last. He had told the truth.

Officer Clark nodded. "Okay, Webber. Why are you telling me this now?" His voice had an edge to it. He sounded more official.

Webb sighed, ran his fingers through his hair. "I had to. I couldn't stand lying about it any longer. I felt like—like I was losing my mind." He appealed to Dylis.

214

"I didn't care anymore about anything, about doing my exercises or getting better. I kept thinking about what I had done, over and over again till I couldn't think of anything else. There wasn't anything else. That's all I was—the person who had run over Taffy Putnam. And I couldn't go on. I didn't want to go on."

Dylis gave a sharp laugh. "But you wanted to be cool. You wanted to eat chili peppers in front of the whole school; you wanted people to think you had been hit by a drunk driver so their hearts would crack open and bleed for you. You didn't want to go on. But you still wanted to be cool."

Webb let out a long sigh. He had known Dylis wouldn't be easy. "I don't blame you for not believing me before," he said. "But believe me now, Dylis. I'm telling the truth," he said earnestly. "I am," he said to Officer Clark.

"I appreciate what you're saying." Officer Clark nodded. "Guilt can ruin your life. I've seen it happen. But what I'm asking"—he exhaled heavily—"is why did you wait until now? Why didn't you tell the truth right after the accident?" He sounded weary.

Webb hesitated. He knew he would be incriminating Grampa, but there was no other way. "I couldn't remember. In the beginning I couldn't remember anything about the accident. Like I told you."

"But your grandfather did?" Officer Clark prompted. "He remembered everything?"

Webb nodded.

"He was trying to protect you. Is that it?"

"Yes." Webb rubbed his palms over his jeans. "He thought he was doing the right thing. He didn't want me to go to jail." He paused. "I—I didn't—I don't want to go to jail. But . . ." He planted one fist on his knee and brought his other fist down on top of it. "I'd rather go to jail than have my grampa go for something I did. I want to own up to what I did, take my own punishment."

Officer Clark stood up and walked around the room. He walked over to the window and pulled back one of the flimsy drapes with his hand. It was dark outside. A streetlight made a circle of light in the middle of the intersection. The lamp swayed in the wind, pulling and pushing the circle back and forth. He let go of the drape and walked back across the floor, pausing to pet the cat, which sank down under his hand like a gray puddle. He walked over to the aquarium and squatted, watching the fish like he had forgotten all about Webb.

Finally Dylis said, "Dad."

He came back and sat down. To Webb he said, "I want you to take me through it all again. From the moment you got in the car with your grandfather to the moment of impact. The very beginning to the very end."

Webb talked for fifteen minutes, recalling tiny details like the way the sunlight struck the top half of a billboard on Midline Road advertising suntan lotion. The sound of his knuckles striking the hood when he walked around the front of the car, the song on the radio.

"Do you remember the words?" Officer Clark asked.

Webb remembered. The song was as familiar to him now as an old lullaby. " 'Lay it down, oh, lay it down,' " he began, " 'put it with forgotten things, it will rise, oh, it will rise—' "

" 'Like the bird with silver wings.' " Dylis finished the last line.

They both looked at her for a moment; then Officer Clark motioned for Webb to continue. When he was done, Officer Clark picked up a pencil from the table and rolled it back and forth between the palms of his hands. "So what do you want, Webber? Why are you coming to me with this story?"

Webb gave him a stricken look, and he held up his hand. "I believe you. But what do you want to do now?"

"I wanted to tell you so you can change the record, the deposition, whatever. If anyone is punished, it will be me, not my grandfather. I'll go to jail if I have to. And if they sue my mother . . ." He shook his head. "I don't know. That's the part I don't know. If they understood that my mother has nothing to do with this, that she doesn't have much money . . . I mean, do you think they'll sue me? Not that they don't deserve more money," he added quickly.

"No, Webber." Officer Clark shook his head. "I don't think they're going to sue you. Because they still think your grandfather hit Taffy."

"But after you change the deposition—"

"The only one who can do that is your grandfather. He gave his testimony as the truth. We have no other proof."

"But he was protecting me. He didn't want me to go to jail."

Officer Clark smiled. "No one is going to jail. There was no reckless driving, no speeding, no one was drinking."

"No jail?" Webb leaned forward. "For sure?"

"I can almost guarantee it." Officer Clark picked up the pencil again and started rapping it across the backs of his knuckles. "Look, Webber, I don't think you're going to change anything. The car is in your grandfather's name, isn't it?" When Webb nodded he went on, "No matter who was driving, he's liable. If anyone is sued, it will be him. Are you sure you want to go through with this?"

"Dad!" Dylis jumped off the sofa and pointed at Webb. "He's the one who ran over Taffy. He's been lying for five months. Are you going to let him off the hook just like that?"

Officer Clark half-smiled. "Dylis." He shook his head. "Webber will never be off the hook. He knows what he did." He looked back at Webb. "You're not going to change anything, Webber," he said again. "Not unless your grandfather retracts his statement."

Webb sat there staring at the braided rug, listening to the burbling fish tank. He had tried to tell the truth, and it didn't make any difference. After everything he had been through, it didn't make any difference. Grampa would never change his story, even if he knew there was no jail sentence, even if he knew Webb wouldn't get sued. So why not let it go? It would be so simple, he thought. "Do you think I should . . . let it go?" he asked slowly.

Officer Clark didn't answer for a moment. He rapped the pencil eraser against the table. "It *would* be the simplest thing," he said at last.

Webb looked over at Dylis, who was standing with her back to them now, her square, stubborn figure in its familiar pose, arms crossed in front of her, mad at the world. She was staring into the fish tank. He knew she wanted to pick up the tank and hurl it at both of them. He understood her a little now after all these months. She wanted the world to be safe for dolphins and everything else. She wanted people to follow the rules and behave nicely even when no one was looking. If they did something wrong, they should own up to it. Even if it was something terrible. She was a pain in the butt, the self-appointed conscience of the whole world.

"I can't let it go," he said finally. "Dylis wouldn't like it."

Dylis turned around and stared at him. Webb looked back.

"Are you serious?" Officer Clark asked.

"Yes, I am." Webb nodded vigorously.

"Okay, Webber. I'll see this through with you."

He shook Webb's hand at the door. "You've got guts, I'll say that for you."

Dylis came forward pushing her hair back with one hand. "You're crazy," she said gruffly.

Webb nodded. "Yeah," he said. "I couldn't have done it without you."

Before he went out the door he looked back. Dylis was gazing at him, almost smiling. She gave him an awkward wave. Then he stepped outside into the chilly night, hands in his pockets, and limped over to the circle of light. He stood there looking down Pacific Street, breathing deeply of the frosty air. Taking his hands out of his pockets, he started to run. His stride was clumsy and off balance. Looking at him, nobody would guess that he was once the pride of Spratling High. But in his mind, Webb was flying.

chapter 20

WEBB OPENED the kitchen door and smelled burned meat. He went to the stove and lifted the lid of the cast-iron pot. Inside was a crust of hardened, scorched stew. He turned off the burner. How long had it been on?

"Grampa?" There was no answer. He looked at the table set for three, the wooden bowl in the center filled with tossed salad. Were Grampa and his mother out looking for him? He should have called, he thought, hurrying forward into the darkened living room. "Where are they?" he muttered. "What time is it, anyhow?" He was about to hit the switch on the wall when, in the light coming from outside, he spotted Grampa stretched out on the sofa, wearing his white apron over his shirt and black pants. His hands were folded across his chest.

Webb went down on his knees. "Grampa!" He grabbed him by the shoulders and shook him. "Grampa!"

Grampa groaned and opened his eyes. He blinked and looked at Webb. "What's wrong?"

Webb sank back on the floor and blew out a long breath. "What are you doing like this—in the dark, all alone? Geez, don't scare me." He shook his head. "Why are you sleeping? Where's Mom?"

"Finishing somebody's drapes," Grampa mumbled. "Be home late." He sat up and smoothed down his beard. Then he sniffed the air. "My stew!" He grabbed at the sofa arm as if to get up, but Webb eased him back down.

"Forget it. The stew's petrified. You left the burner on." Webb sat down beside him on the sofa.

"Damn." Grampa slapped his knee. "Two pounds of lamb. I was just going to stretch out here for a minute. Bahhh." He hit his forehead. "Look at this. Laid out like I'm ready for the glue factory."

"It's my fault," Webb said. "I'm late. I . . ." He faltered and cleared his throat. "I should have called."

Grampa turned to the clock glowing red on top of the TV. "It's almost eight." He looked back at Webb, frowning. "Where were you until this hour of the night?"

All the way home Webb had thought about what he

was going to say to Grampa and Mom over the dinner table. This would have been easier with his mother there. She would have been with him, would have supported his decision. But now it was only Grampa. How could Webb ever make him understand? "Grampa—"

"What?" Grampa leaned forward eagerly and smoothed down Webb's collar. "What is it, Boomer?"

Webber had a sudden memory of the afternoon he told Grampa about running the sixteen hundred in four-thirty. He remembered holding back for a minute, anticipating Grampa's excitement at his news. Now it almost seemed they had come around full circle— Grampa's lined, droopy face lifted in anticipation. If only he could stay in this moment, Webb thought, with Grampa's eyes fixed on him, trusting in him, trusting in his love. If they could just stay like this forever. He swallowed and reached over to take Grampa's hand. "Grampa," he said again.

"What? Tell me." Grampa sat forward, sensing something.

Webb shifted on the sofa, facing Grampa more squarely. He took a deep breath. "I went to . . . I went to that policeman's house tonight. I went to . . . to Officer Clark's house and—"

Grampa sat back with a jerk as if Webb had slapped him. "What are you saying?"

"Just listen to me, Grampa. I went to his house," Webb said again, "and I—I told him everything. Everything."

"Wait a minute, wait a minute, wait a minute." Grampa put his hands to his chest and stared at Webb. He opened his mouth, but nothing came out. He just sat there staring. The smell of ruined stew hung in the silence between them. Outside, a siren wailed down Scott Street, past the house, and around the corner. Neither of them said anything until it faded away. Then it was Webb who spoke.

"I had to do it, Grampa. I couldn't live with it anymore."

Grampa shook his head. "No. This can't be true. I don't believe it. Why would you ruin your life?" He stood up, not taking his eyes off Webb, like he could hold him there with his eyes alone. "You talked to this policeman? What's his number? I'm going to look it up." He started for the telephone. "I'll call him, explain that it was a mistake. You were trying to protect me."

"Grampa!" Webb stood up, his concern turning to anger. "I know what I'm doing. Stay out of it. Just stay out of it, for a change. You're the one who made the mistake—trying to take the blame for what I did. Do you think you can fix everything with another lie?"

"Another lie? Another lie?" Grampa yelled. "Don't get all high and mighty on me, Webber. A little lie is not the end of the world. A little lie—what is it?" He waved his arm. "A nothing," he said, the color rising in his face. "And you're a fool if you think you're taking the high road by spilling your guts. This isn't going to make anything better—it's going to make it worse.

Worse," he repeated, pointing at Webber. "You have no idea, no godforsaken idea, Webber, what the hell you're doing. You're a fool, Webber." He stood there gasping, the veins throbbing in his neck.

Webb jumped to his feet and struck the wall over the sofa with his fist. "You're the idiot!" he shouted back. "You keep pushing me down and pushing me down like I'm some kind of—puppet. Maybe you can fool Officer Clark and maybe you can fool Taffy Putnam, but you can't fool me. I know what I did. I—I know every dirty little detail of that accident, everything, everything. I ruined someone's life. I'm supposed to keep going to school, going to parties, laugh at jokes, be this big-shot track star? You don't know, you don't know, Grampa!" He was waving his arms and yelling, turning back and forth on his good leg. "Maybe you can live with it, maybe even Taffy Putnam can live with it. But I can't. I'm not a machine. I'm not a puppet. I have to live with me the rest of my life. And me is the person who got behind the wheel of that car like a brainless fifteen-year-old jerk, not paying attention, and ran over a little girl who will spend the rest of her life in a wheelchair. You don't understand—no matter where I put my eyes, no matter how fast I run, I'm still that jerk. You can't fool me, Grampa. A little lie! For me, it's the end of the world." His voice was shaking.

Grampa stared at him, panting. "You don't know what this means," he said slowly.

"No, I don't," Webb burst out. "I know I'm not

going to jail—I know that much. I'm not even going to get sued. But if you get sued, it's my debt. Maybe I'll have to work the rest of my life to pay it off. I don't know."

"But you can handle it, Mr. Big Shot?"

Webb looked at him. "I'm trying to do the right thing. Why are you making it so hard for me?"

"Because," Grampa said, lifting his hands imploringly, "it's not the right thing. It's the wrong thing. It's the worst thing. Listen to me. I can save you. I can still save you. You've got to listen to me, Boomer. It's the one thing I can do before I die. Maybe, after I'm gone, then you can tell the truth to your children, to your grandchildren. Tell the whole world. Tell them Grampa was ready to lay down his life for you." He sank wearily to the sofa. "Please, sweetheart."

"No!" Webb yelled. "You're not doing it for me. You want to be this big legend that everyone talks about. Riding into the valley of death and all that crap. I can't make you a hero. Go put out another damn fire if you want to be such a big shot!" Webb turned away, pressing both hands into the wall. Finally he took a deep breath and turned around. "I know you would lay down your life for me," he said in a softer tone. "Everyone knows that about you. That you would do anything for me. That you would go to jail for me, even."

Grampa shrugged.

"I'm asking you to do this for me, Grampa. For you,

maybe it's even harder than dying for me. But it's what I want. It's what I want more than anything."

Grampa looked up at him wearily.

Webb dropped to the floor and put his arms around Grampa's legs, feeling how spindly they were under the worn fabric. "Remember *The Alamo*? Where John Wayne says you might be walking around but you're dead as a beaver hat?" Webb gave a dry laugh. "For five months I've been like a beaver hat. I want to live again, Grampa. I've got to do this even if my life isn't perfect. I have to." He drew in a long breath. "I want you to call Officer Clark and tell him the truth."

Grampa snorted. "You want me to tell everyone that I was only covering up for you so I could take the blame for the accident and that now I've changed my mind? Now I want you to take the blame. Is that right?" He looked Webb in the eye.

"But it's the truth. It's the right thing to do. You know it is."

"Puhh." Grampa batted the air with his hand. "I try to save you and then I turn you in. Would anyone think that's the right thing to do? How would that look? 'Grandfather tosses grandson to the wolves'—that's what they'd write about me. Never. I will never."

"Don't you get it? This is not about you, Grampa! It's about me."

"Your precious conscience," Grampa muttered.

In that moment Webb began to understand Grampa

227

as he saw himself—an old man who lived off the good-will of his daughter-in-law, who puttered around the house in an apron, cooking meatloaf and salmon patties. If Webb gave in, Grampa's life would be fulfilled some-how. He could die happy, knowing that he had sacri-ficed himself for Webb, that he would live on in this deed like some mythic hero. It was probably the only real gift Webb could give and that Grampa could accept in their entire lives together. If he could just let it go.

Sitting there on the living room floor, with the wind beating the new buds of the forsythia against the win-dow, Webb had a memory of another windy March day. For a reason he didn't quite understand, he started talking. "Do you remember, Grampa, that first day at Fatty's Funland—you bought me that gold plastic hat? It said FATTY'S FUNLAND FOREVER. I felt like such a big cheese, walking through those mobs of people, sure that everyone was admiring me in my gold hat." Webb smiled at the memory.

"Then we went for some cotton candy and when you were paying for it, the wind picked the hat off my head and carried it right up through the air like a kite. All I could think about was how I felt with the hat on and how I had to get it back. So I took off running, shoving my way through all these people, trying to see where my hat went, and I spotted it on the ground by the Ferris wheel. And it was okay—nobody had stepped on it or anything. But before I could get over there, a kid—older than me, with a bunch of his friends—picked it up and started to get in a seat for the Ferris wheel. I yelled that it was my hat, that my grampa just bought it for me, but he and his friends laughed. He put the hat on and they all got on the Ferris wheel, just laughing their guts out. When the Ferris wheel took off, I could see my hat go way up over my head, getting smaller and smaller. And I knew it was gone.

"And then I looked around and realized you were gone too, that I didn't have a clue where the cotton candy stand was." Webb laughed and shook his head.

"God, I was scared, Grampa. I can still remember the feeling of being surrounded by all these people pushing by me, laughing, eating, and I felt like a—like a two-year-old or something. Except people would have noticed a two-year-old stumbling around all alone. Nobody noticed me standing there hunched up behind the big, cruddy engine of the Ferris wheel, trying not to cry, trying not to be scared. I lost my father, I lost my gold hat, and then I lost you. It was all over for me. Nobody cared. Nobody would even bother to come looking for me. I would be stuck there, hungry and cold, at Fatty's Funland forever.

"I don't know how long I stood there behind that engine, studying this big, stinking gray box like it was my fortune or something. But then I looked up. I don't know why—I just looked up over the heads of all these people, across the park, and there you were. You were standing on the bench of the merry-go-round, with your legs braced against the back of the seat. And you were holding these two cones of cotton candy up in the air like torches. You were going around and around, squinting into the crowd and yelling. I couldn't hear you because of the noise, but I knew what you were saying. You didn't care if people were laughing at you standing up there," Webb said, looking up into Grampa's face. "I knew it then. You would never leave me."

Webb sighed, his anger gone. His love for Grampa would always be deeper than anger, than sorrow or regret. "Maybe you didn't go off to war," he went on, "or rescue someone from a burning building. I don't care about those things. What I care about is that every day when I came home from school, you were sitting at the kitchen table, waiting to hear everything I did that day, like it was more important than what the President of the United States did. And every track meet I was ever in, you were there. Even if I couldn't see you, I could feel you pulling for me. Even when you kissed me in front of my friends, I knew it was because you loved me more than you loved anyone in the world." Webb took Grampa's hand. "Grampa the Great." He looked up at Grampa and laughed.

Grampa only sighed and waved the words away.

"I have to do it, Grampa," Webb said. "I have to tell Mom. I have to tell the Putnams. Everyone. You know it's right, Grampa."

"No," Grampa said in a trembling voice. "Never."

Webb laid his head on Grampa's knee. He was so

tired he ached, as tired as if he had run a thousand miles. He wrapped his arms around Grampa's legs and closed his eyes. Gently Grampa laid his hands on Webb's head. And they listened to their breathing in the dark.

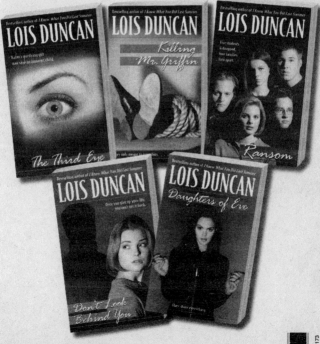